W9-CBD-164

Take a Chance, Gramps!

BOOKS BY JEAN DAVIES OKIMOTO

Novels:
My Mother Is Not Married to My Father
It's Just Too Much
Norman Schnurman, Average Person
Who Did It, Jenny Lake?
Jason's Women
Molly by Any Other Name

Picture Books:
Blumpoe the Grumpoe Meets Arnold the Cat

Short Stories:
"Jason the Quick and the Brave"
"Moonbeam Dawson and the Killer Bear"

One-Act Play:
Hum It Again, Jeremy

Nonfiction:
Boomerang Kids: How to Live with
Adult Children Who Return Home

Take a Chance, Gramps!

Jean Davies Okimoto

Little, Brown and Company

Boston   Toronto   London

Copyright © 1990 by Jean D. Okimoto

All rights reserved. No part of this book may be reproduced in any form or by any electronic or mechanical means, including information storage and retrieval systems, without permission in writing from the publisher, except by a reviewer who may quote brief passages in a review.

First Edition

The characters and events in this book are fictitious. Any similarity to real persons, living or dead, is coincidental and not intended by the author.

Library of Congress Cataloging-in-Publication Data

Okimoto, Jean Davies.
    Take a chance, Gramps! / by Jean Davies Okimoto. — 1st ed.
        p.   cm.
    Summary: Twelve-year-old Jane and her grandfather, both of whom have suffered losses, help each other reach out, make new friends, and change their lives.
    ISBN 0-316-63812-9 (HC)
    [1. Grandfather — Fiction.   2. Friendship — Fiction.   3. Loss (Psychology) — Fiction.]   I. Title.
PZ7.O415Tak   1990
[Fic] — dc20   90-6499

Joy Street Books are published by
Little, Brown and Company (Inc.)

10 9 8 7 6 5 4 3

HC

Published simultaneously in Canada
by Little, Brown & Company (Canada) Limited

Printed in the United States of America

For Bob and Trish

Take a Chance, Gramps!

One

"Janie!" Mom shrieked, "TELEPHONE!" Her face was bright red, and she was dripping with sweat as she poked her head around the corner.

I trotted down the hall, glancing in at Gramps as I went by. As usual, he was just sitting in his room slumped in his chair. I wished I could do something; it made me sad about Gramps.

In Mom's room I picked up the phone. I knew it was Alicia, even though she didn't sound like herself at all. She sounded awful.

"Alicia? What's wrong?"

"Can I come over?" She choked out the words.

"Sure. Come on — I'll be here." I jammed myself in the corner, facing the walls, and squished my hand on my ear, pretending I was in a phone booth. I get claustrophobia using the phone in my parents' room, especially with Mom riding her exercise bike in the corner. I've been trying to convince her that I need an extension in my room, but she thinks our present phone situation is perfectly satisfactory. To me it is perfectly unsatisfactory.

It's perfectly crummy; I could hardly hear Alicia, between the wheels' whizzing and squeaking and Mom's puffing and panting.

"Alicia, what happened?"

No answer. Just sniffling.

"Want to wait to tell when you get here?"

"Yes," she said between loud sniffs.

"Maybe we should meet at the tree?"

"Okay." She sniffed again and hung up.

I knew something terrible must have happened. Alicia Haglund, my best friend since the fifth grade, is not the kind of person who falls apart easily. I looked at my watch; I'd have to leave in exactly eight minutes. We called it the Higgins-Haglund Precision Meeting System; if I left eight minutes after we hung up, and she left two minutes after she hung up, we'd meet at the tree in the park between our houses at exactly the same time. We had it down cold.

"Is everything all right?" Mom gasped, wiping her forehead on the shoulder of her T-shirt. "Was it Alicia?"

I nodded. Actually, I wondered who else Mom thought it could be; no one ever calls me except Alicia.

"She sounded as if she has a cold. Is she sick?" Mom asked. Then she started pedaling like a maniac. I guess she had slowed down while I was on the phone so the bike wouldn't be loud. It hadn't helped.

"No, something's really wrong. She was crying."

"Well, I hope it's nothing big," Mom said, wiggling from side to side, her knees flying up and down.

The minute Mom said that, I got worried. "What if someone in her family has a terrible disease — *and there's no hope?*"

"What?" Outside, Dad had started up the lawn mower. He must have been right under the window; it sounded

4

as if he were mowing the bedroom rug instead of the yard.

"I SAID, 'MAYBE SOMEONE IN HER FAMILY HAS A TERRIBLE DISEASE.' "

"JANIE, I DON'T THINK —" Finally Dad headed across the yard. "Janie, I don't think speculating will do any good," Mom continued, trying to talk in her normal voice, although she was panting after every word. "Try-to-think-it's-something-small," she gasped, leaning forward on the handle bars, completely wasted.

I tried to think of some small things it could be while I left Mom's room; but I couldn't imagine even a middle-sized disaster that would make Alicia sound that miserable.

As I headed past my brother's room, he poked his head out the doorway. "Hey, Janie, come here — look at this one! It's great! I know this will get us on the show," he hollered.

I checked my watch: precisely six minutes until departure. "Okay, but it'll have to be quick. I hope it's better than when you tied that American flag to her tail, and she was supposed to wag in time to the 'Star Spangled Banner.' "

"That trick wasn't so bad."

"The flag flew off before you got to the 'dawn's early light.' "

"The tricks are supposed to be stupid," John said seriously.

"Not that stupid."

"Stupid pet tricks. That's exactly what they want on the David Letterman show."

"I know, silly, but they have to be *good* stupid pet tricks. The pet has to do the trick right. When that flag kept flying off, it wasn't —"

5

"Okay, okay. But just watch this — it's great!"

"Go ahead — but make it fast."

"MR. LETTERMAN . . . LADIES . . . AND . . . GENTLEMEN. I BRING YOU . . . JULIET, THE MAGNIFICENT BUBBLE EATER!" My brother presented a bottle of Miracle Bubble, displaying it like a magician. Next he presented the Miracle Wand, grandly waving it around in huge arcs.

"Hurry up, John."

"Okay, okay." He stuck the wand in the gunk, blew on it, and a few bubbles puffed out.

"Woof!" Juliet barked, sprang into the air, and chomped down one of the bubbles.

"Woof woof!" She leaped up and scarfed down two more.

"Woof!" She pounced on another, flew up to bite one floating near John's hand, hit her head on the bottle of Miracle Bubble, and dumped bubble goo all over the floor.

I watched the puddle of Miracle Bubble seeping into John's blue rug. "Great trick."

"Don't tell Mom."

"Don't worry. I have to meet Alicia, anyway. Maybe you should go back to the flag trick again," I advised, heading out the door.

Juliet stepped in the middle of the bubble puddle and followed me out. I still had a couple of minutes before I had to leave, so I went in to see Gramps. Juliet came, too, making little soapy footprints all across his rug on her way to nuzzle him. Juliet and I are a lot alike — we both keep trying with Gramps.

"Hi, Gramps!"

"Buszhbgumph."

"How are you, Gramps?"

"Rrezphrtz bpstzr."

I wished my grandfather would wear his teeth. They just sat in a glass on his dresser. He looked terrible without them, and you couldn't understand anything he said. My grandfather's name is George P. Bliss. Lately, it was more like his name should be George P. Misery. Poor Gramps. He just sat in front of the TV all day with his arms folded across his chest and his teeth out. I don't think he even cared what he was watching. My whole family was worried about him. He came to live with us last January, right after my grandmother died. That's when he stopped wearing his teeth.

"See you later, Gramps." I gave him a cheery wave, but he didn't seem to notice. Juliet trotted after me. She still goes in and sits next to Gramps, even though he never pats her anymore. I never knew a person could change so completely. He used to be crazy about her! If he were his old self, he would have been helping John get Juliet on the David Letterman show. Gramps would have thought up the world's greatest stupid pet trick. He always used to have all kinds of ideas. But now, even though his body still sits there, it's as if he's gone away somewhere. I sure wished I knew how to get him back.

I checked my watch; one minute and thirty seconds. I'd have to fly. The door slammed behind us as Juliet and I rushed out. She always met Alicia at the tree with me. As I ran toward the park, I pretended I was Flo Jo going for the gold, while galloping beside me was Lassie, world-famous film dog. Actually, there's nothing much spectacular about Juliet. Or me, for that matter. We even look alike: medium-brown hair and brown eyes. Juliet is a medium-sized dog, and I am a medium-sized person for being twelve. I guess you might say "plain-Jane" fits me perfectly.

7

When I got to the park, two guys from our sixth-grade class rode by on their bikes, Rick Novito and Ben Caldwell. I wanted to wave, just casually wiggle a few fingers, but by the time I got up the nerve, they had already zoomed past me. It's always like that, but I'm mostly used to it. I don't get noticed unless I'm with Alicia.

I saw her at the edge of the park near McClellan.

"Alicia!" I called to her, waved, and raced toward the tree. Usually Alicia ran, too. But this time she walked so slowly you'd think she was going to the dentist to get all her teeth drilled. I got to the tree way ahead of her. Alicia didn't even wave; she just trudged along looking at the ground.

I leaned back against the trunk. Juliet and I were panting like steam engines. How come Flo Jo seems to take almost regular breaths after a race? I was thinking about Olympic runners and wondering if they have some special way of breathing, but the minute Alicia got close enough so I could see her face, I forgot all about Flo Jo. Alicia looked terrible. Her eyes were all red and bloodshot, and her nose was red and shiny, like a plum.

"Alicia — what happened?"

She just sniffled, plopped down next to me, and leaned back against the trunk.

I patted Juliet, who was practically vibrating from panting. Alicia patted her, too.

"What happened?" I asked again.

"We're moving."

"What?" She was sniffling so much I could hardly understand her.

"We're moving."

"Moving? Who's moving?"

"We are — my family. That's what I'm trying to tell you."

"You mean you're moving to a new house." I wasn't sure what the big deal was.

"Not just a new house. A new city."

"*A new city?*" My heart pounded.

"It's not even in Washington. We're moving to San Jose, California."

"I — I don't believe this —" I mumbled. I felt dazed, like the time I had to play goalie on the Mt. Baker Bombers and the ball kept smacking me in the head. For the second half of the game, I could hardly tell the Bombers from the Lake City Kickettes. I felt like that now. I didn't know what was going on. *I couldn't have heard right.* But as I looked at Alicia's red eyes and her plum nose, I knew I had.

"My parents didn't want to tell me that we might move because they didn't want to upset me for nothing if it didn't happen. My father applied for a new job six months ago. They just found out this morning that he got it."

"But what about school?"

"Mom doesn't want me to have to switch schools after I start, so I'm supposed to go stay with my aunt in San Jose."

"What? You won't start school here? You won't be here a week from next Tuesday?"

Alicia shook her head. "I'm supposed to go to school there with my cousin. Dad's going to be down there, too, and start his job, and then Mom's coming after she sells our house."

"You have to sell your house!"

Alicia nodded again and sniffled some more. "We'll all stay at my aunt's until we buy a new house in San Jose."

I was numb.

I just sat there. Frozen. Then I felt tears running down my cheeks. That made Alicia start sniffling and crying again. I looked over at her. What were we going to do? I had been excited about starting the seventh grade, but nervous, too. Actually superscared is more like it. But at least I wasn't scared alone — I'd always had Alicia.

The two of us had promised to help each other if we got lost trying to find our classrooms. If we felt wimpy being the youngest people in the school, or if we got our period in a class with a man teacher, we said we'd have each other to talk to; and even if we didn't get the same lunch, we knew we could *always* count on sitting together on the bus.

"I hate that your dad did this!" I blurted out, but I felt bad the minute I said it. I looked down at the grass and began picking at it. "Alicia — I'm sorry — I said that about your dad."

"It's okay. I'm mad at him, too."

We sat in silence, as if somebody'd died. I looked at the bottom of the trunk where we had carved our names last summer. Some moss was growing in the "A" and the "L."

"I wonder if there are any cute guys in San Jose?" I said, finally.

"I don't know. My cousin says so."

"What's she like?"

"I don't know. I haven't seen her since second grade — I don't even remember her. I hope she's not a nerd. That's all I'd need starting out there — is getting stuck with a nerd."

"That'd be the worst." I agreed. How terrible if that happened to Alicia. But then it hit me — there wasn't *anyone* for me to get stuck with!

For the past two years, in fifth and in sixth grade, I'd

spent every second with Alicia. I knew other people at school, but they were just people you knew, not people you'd count on. One time I even decided that if you had just one friend to be with, you could stand watching *Friday the Thirteenth* on Halloween night in a dark house with your parents out. You could scream together and hug each other during the scary parts, and everything would be okay. That's all you need for most things, just one friend. That's what I always believed. I never thought about what would happen if the one friend moved!

I didn't have a cousin or even a single person from sixth grade I could call up. I felt like a soccer ball had clobbered me in the stomach. I felt like I had lost my best friend. And I realized . . . *I had. My best and only friend.*

Two

*

I thought I would be able to spend every minute of every day with Alicia before she left. We'd check out the lifeguards while splashing around at the beach, go downtown to slobber over the clothes at Nordstrom's, call up KZOK to dedicate songs to guys in our class, watch Alicia's video of *The Karate Kid* for the hundredth time, hang out at the park to spot cute guys in our class, whack the ball around the tennis courts, and devour Chocolate Decadence cake at the Pacific Dessert Company. I thought it would be a wonderful whirlwind of all our favorite things.

I thought wrong.

Alicia had to help her mom clean the house and get it ready for the people from the Golden Door Real Estate Company. If I wanted to be with her I had to go over and scrub. The only thing fantastic about our last three days together was the Fantastik spray cleaner.

But at least I got to go with her family to the airport to see her off. Her mom had invited me while I was mopping their bathroom. The night before Alicia left, when I was sure Mom, Dad, John, and Gramps were asleep, I tiptoed down to the kitchen. That's where Juliet sleeps. She has a burlap bag filled with cedar shavings that's supposed to make her not smell. It doesn't work. I sat on the floor next to her and patted her for a few minutes. Then I carefully snuck her up to my room. Juliet's not allowed on the furniture, so I tried not to make a sound as I lifted her, gently putting her under the covers, except for her head, which was on the pillow next to mine. It doesn't bother me that she stinks.

"It's going to be a terrible day tomorrow, Juliet," I whispered. "Alicia's leaving."

Juliet licked my face.

"She's leaving for good," I whispered. Juliet licked me some more. Dog germs don't bother me. Juliet seemed very happy. I think she liked my bed better than the burlap bag. I guess I finally fell asleep, because I don't remember how long I lay there, telling her about tomorrow, the most dreaded day of my life.

In the morning, when I woke up, I had a knot in my stomach. It's the kind of knot I get when I'm mad at someone, and the person I was mad at was Alicia. I know it wasn't fair; it wasn't her fault, but I was mad at her for leaving.

I got dressed and went downstairs to the kitchen, taking Juliet with me. I was pounding the burlap bag to make it look like she had slept there, when Mom came in.

"Jane! What're you doing to Juliet's bed?"

"Sometimes you just feel like hitting something, Mom."

"I know, honey. But instead of punching that bag — why don't you let me fix you a nice breakfast." I knew she was really trying to be nice, because she was on a diet, and she hardly ever cooks when she's dieting.

"How about some waffles?"

"No, thanks."

"Pancakes?"

I shook my head.

"French toast? Bacon and eggs?" Mom swung open the refrigerator door. "I know — an omelet!" She must have been getting desperate. She doesn't even like eating omelets, let alone cooking them.

"I'll just have some cereal, I guess."

Mom made herself a cup of coffee and sat next to me.

"You'll get over this, Janie." She reached over and patted my hand. "I know you don't believe me now, honey, but you will, really you will. You'll make new friends."

She was right, I didn't believe her. And even if I did, how was that supposed to help right now — or worse, the day after Labor Day, when I had to start seventh grade without Alicia? I heard a car honk. "That must be the Haglunds." I grabbed my jeans jacket and my purse. "Bye, Mom."

Mr. and Mrs. Haglund were sitting in the front seat; it's a two-door car, and Mrs. Haglund held open the door while she tipped her seat forward.

"Hurry up, dear," she said. She was tipped so far forward, her head was practically jammed between the dashboard and the windshield. I tried to hurry, but I had to squish in the back with Alicia and her grandparents, and I was trying not to step on their feet. I smushed in next to Alicia's grandmother. As soon as Mrs. Haglund shut the door, I started coughing.

"Are you all right, dear?" Alicia's mother asked.

"Co-could you roll down the window?" I gasped. Alicia's grandmother had on this very strong perfume and the whole car stunk.

"Just a wee bit. I don't want to mess up my hair," her grandmother said sweetly as she patted her blue hair, then my knee.

Mrs. Haglund opened the window a crack, and I stuck my nose out like a dog, wishing I had never come. I rode the whole way to the airport like that. Alicia was on the other side of her grandparents, and we never said a word.

Most of the time Alicia's grandparents were a lot of fun and very energetic. Her grandmother went to aerobics, and her grandfather played tennis every day. Once in a while I felt sad when I was around them, because they were how Gramps used to be, but usually I liked to talk to them. Not today. I didn't like them or anybody in that car very much, except for Alicia; and I was still a little mad at her for deserting me.

"Looks like a good day to fly," Alicia's grandfather said when we got on the freeway.

No one said anything.

"Janie, you can visit us someday in San Jose," her dad said. Then he started singing, *Do you know the way to San Jose — da-da-da-da.*"

"*Da-dad-da-da —*" Alicia's mother joined in and looked in the back seat and smiled at us.

"*Do you know the way to San Jose — da-da-da-da —*" they both sang cheerfully.

Then her grandmother flipped open her purse. Oh, no! She squirted more perfume on from this little spray thing she had in there. Yuk. I thought I was going to throw up. The second we got to the airport, I practically flattened Alicia's grandmother as I scrambled out of the car to get some air. I walked around taking deep breaths, breathing all over the place, while they unloaded the bags.

We had to wait about a half hour at the gate until the plane came. I looked down at the floor, then over at Alicia. She was staring at the newsstand. Looking at each other was too hard; I was afraid I'd start crying, and I think she was afraid of the same thing. I glanced over at her grandmother, and she was dabbing her eyes with a handkerchief. Her grandfather had a newspaper in front of his face, but every few minutes he'd put it down and blow his nose. I wondered if they were mad at her dad, too.

"Here's my address at my aunt's." Alicia opened her purse, handed me a slip of paper, then stared at the newsstand again.

On the top of the paper it said, "WRITE OR ELSE — HA! HA!" Underneath that it had Alicia's new address. I folded it up and put it in my pocket.

"Do you have mine?" I mumbled.

"Janie," she said, "are you kidding? I'll remember my whole life that you live on 3363 Court Street!"

"I'll write every day."

"I will, too."

"Maybe you could come back for a visit?"

"Mom said we'll be back at Christmas to visit my grandparents."

"But that's five whole months away!"

Finally, passengers herded together to board and Alicia's parents stood up and everyone started grabbing each other. Her grandparents even hugged me, and I wasn't going anywhere. I guess they got a little carried away.

"I'll see you at Christmas," I said, hugging Alicia hard.

"Here —" She took my hand and put a little box in it.

"What's this?"

"It's about the 'M' word," she whispered.

"Thanks." Then I did start crying. I didn't even have to open the box. I knew what it was.

"Don't do anything I wouldn't do."

"Alicia — let's just pretend you're going away for the weekend."

"Okay." Alicia walked to the gate with her father. While the flight attendant checked their tickets, she turned and waved. She had a smile on her face while tears ran down her cheeks. "Bye, Janie. See you Monday."

I waved back. "Bye. Have — have a great weekend. See you — Monday." I wanted to smile the way Alicia had, but I couldn't. Maybe I could only do one thing at a time. Right then, it was cry.

On the way home I sat in the back seat with Alicia's grandfather. Her grandmother and her mother were in the front. Her mother chattered away about the real estate people coming, yabity, yabity, yabity, while the rest of us just sat there like stones. At least there wasn't any singing. I peeked in the box. Just as I thought, it was one of Alicia's mother's lipsticks — a gorgeous pink one. I looked on the bottom. Watermelon Magic — I loved it. Mrs. Haglund always let us fool around with her makeup, but no way could we do it at my house. "Sixth grade is too young for makeup. I simply don't approve, Jane," my mother said the first time I came downstairs wearing lipstick. The next time I tried it, a few months later, I got this whole speech about how it's shallow and superficial for girls to spend so much time trying to be pretty. My mother would pounce on any opportunity she could to convince me makeup was a waste of time. "If women spent as much time on their brains as their bodies, maybe they wouldn't make sixty-four cents for every dollar a man makes," Mom would say when she was really on a roll. Even a Revlon commercial could set her off. When I told Alicia that I had heard the old shallow-superficial speech for the sixteenth time, she came up with the idea of calling makeup the "M" word when we were at my house. I thought it was a fine idea.

By the time I got home, it was raining. I let myself in and went up to my room. I could hear Mom and Dad talking about Gramps again. I was glad my Dad isn't like Alicia's. He doesn't try to be a comedian singing da-da-da-da-*dum* songs. He listens to me, and he's very calm. The only time I remember he got crazy was when he quit smoking. He yelled at Mom because he couldn't find his socks, he yelled at me and John for noisy cereal eating, he yelled at Juliet because she smells, he even yelled at the plants for turning brown. When parents go on health programs, it's usually bad for the kids. But except for the time he quit smoking, Dad is easy to talk to. Mom mostly is, too. But she also always has a zillion solutions for me. She's the one who makes things go in our family. I felt very crummy right then, and it might have helped to talk to either one of them, but they were both so involved in talking about Gramps that I decided not to bother them.

In my room, I put on a little of the Watermelon Magic lipstick, practiced smiling in the mirror a few times, then wiped it off and put it in the back of my underwear drawer.

After a while it quit raining, so I decided to ride my

bike to the park. I wanted to write to Alicia, but there was nothing to say. All I could say would be:

Dear Alicia,
I came home from the airport, went to
the bathroom, and I tried on the
lipstick. I miss you. I'm miserable.
                                        Love,
                                        Janie

Who'd want to read that? At least maybe there'd be something interesting at the park. I was getting my bike out when I heard all this giggling from the top of the garage.

"Watch out! It's the blooey grunt!"

"Ha ha ha. The blooey grunt's here!"

It was my brother and Kevin Wong, one of his millions of friends. Dad says John has more friends than a dog has fleas. I'm like a dog with one flea, at least I used to be. John has a fort that he made in the attic of the garage. I have no idea what he does up there all the time, except get into laughing fits. These days he thinks everything that has to do with the bathroom is hilarious. All one of his friends has to do is say "toilet," or better yet, "toilet paper," and they crack up. They have all kinds of secret words; blooey grunt was their latest. I suppose stuff like that is funny if you're in the fourth grade. I have a word for him and it's no secret. Ridiculous!

"Beware of the blooey grunt!"

"Shut up, scum."

Just as I yelled, my mom stuck her head out the kitchen window. "Jane! Come in here."

It's guaranteed — whenever I yell back at my brother, that's exactly when my mom tunes in. Boy, did she sound uptight! A lot more than usual. In fact, she had seemed a little weird lately. This began when she got the invitation to her twentieth high-school reunion. She'd kind of been bouncing around, which was very unusual for her. My mom is a very reliable and dependable person. She doesn't like anything the least bit unusual — that's why she named me Jane and my brother John. Mom says that when you come from a family like hers, where the whole group sounds like a flower garden, you want things to be ordinary. My Mom's name is Lily, and her sisters are named Rose, Violet, and Daisy.

Mom was in the kitchen, peeling vegetables. She'd been on a diet called the vegetable diet; every day she ate a different one. She got to eat all she wanted, but only that vegetable. She also took special vitamins and drank goo she made from powdered stuff. It looked disgusting. And she'd been riding that exercise bike like crazy. Mom said she had to lose ten pounds before September 28th, when she left for her reunion in Indiana.

I watched her peel the carrots. Slash! Ten of 'em were peeled in a second. Bam! Bam! Bam! She chopped those carrots in neat little pieces. Whap! She picked them all up and dumped them in a bowl. It must be like that when she's at work. Mom is an emergency-room nurse at St. Cabrini Hospital. That's how reliable she is. My mom is exactly the kind of person who can handle emergencies. Although I've never seen her in the operating room, I know she'd be outstanding. I can just see her. The doctor would say, "Scalpel!" and BAM! she'd whip it out — right away — no fumbling, and then he or *she* (Mom has made a very big deal my whole life of telling me that girls can do anything) would say, "Cotton balls!" and BAM! like lightning, my mom would stuff his or *her* hand full of 'em, or, "Wipe up that blood!" and whooosh — it'd be gone, just like that. Mom just does everything right; nothing ever seems to rattle her. That's why it was so strange the way she'd been acting about her high-school reunion.

"Jane, I've got to talk to you." Mom stuck the bowl of carrots in the refrigerator.

"I'm sick of him calling me a blooey grunt all the time."

"No, not that. It's about Gramps."

"What about him?" I felt a knot in my stomach the minute she said that. It was hard to imagine that things could be worse for him, but what if something had happened?

"You know Dad and I are very worried about him — I know you are, too." Mom wiped her hands and sat down at the kitchen table.

I just nodded.

"I want you to help."

"Me? What can I do?"

"I want you to get Gramps out of the house. I want you to take the bus downtown with him Saturday and get on the monorail and ride to Seattle Center with him."

"Seattle Center? Just me and Gramps?"

"Janie, he needs to get out of the house and go somewhere that's full of life, where there's a lot to see and do. Best of all, Seattle Center is filled with lots of people of all ages."

"Gramps used to love Seattle Center. He always bragged that he was there when it was first built for the World's Fair, in 1962."

"That's why Dad and I thought it might be just what

he needs, but we can't persuade him to go there or anywhere else with us. We thought he might be more receptive to going with you. He's always had such a soft spot in his heart for you, honey."

"Oh. Well, I guess I could try — do you want me to ask him?"

"I thought I'd be the one to ask him." Mom crossed her fingers and smiled. "This could really work if I can convince him that by taking you he's helping out."

"Like he's doing me a favor?"

"Yes, sort of like that."

"Sure, I'll sign up for your scheme, Mom. Anything to help Gramps."

I didn't want to tell her because she had so much hope for it, but truthfully, I didn't think Mom's plan would work. Gramps wanted to do things with me before Gramma died, but not anymore. When I went in his room, he didn't even want to talk to me, so I sure couldn't see him taking me to Seattle Center!

I went back out to the garage and got my bike, this time without being called a blooey grunt. As I rode down the block, I saw our next-door neighbor, Dr. Harriett Heedlemaker, working in her yard. Whenever I see her, I have the urge to jump in the bushes. There's a good reason for this. Dr. Heedlemaker is a researcher at the University of Washington. Last year she was working on a project called the "Masculinization of First-born Girls." Her idea was that fathers want sons first, so when they get a daughter instead of a son, they try to turn her into a boy. Since I am the oldest kid in my family, and since I am a girl, she picked me to do research on. My mom said since it was in the interest of science, it was okay, even though she doesn't like Dr. Heedlemaker much. Mom says Harriett Heedlemaker is arrogant and elitist, whatever that is. I just think she's weird.

I didn't have to do anything except "be observed," but this meant I got followed around by Dr. Harriett Heedlemaker for almost a month! Everywhere I went, she'd be right on my heels, scribbling away in a little notebook, or tailing me in her brown Volvo station wagon. Alicia and I used to call her Dr. Needlehead; we did everything we could to ditch her, climbing trees and jumping into the bushes, but she'd always pop up. Even though her research project has been over for a long time, every time I see her, I think, "Eat my dust, Needlehead," and I make a quick getaway.

When I got to Mt. Baker Park, I looked around. The park was pretty quiet, except for some people playing tennis. Actually, they weren't just people, they were guys. I took a closer look and practically went into shock when I realized it was Darrell Williams and Brian Kimura. Last year in my sixth-grade class, they were shrimpy and pudgy — now I could hardly believe my eyes! Mom would say they had a growth spurt over the summer. I'd say it was more like a gorgeous spurt! I was a nervous wreck. It's one thing to be around boys when you're with your best friend, who can and does talk to anybody without turning red and stammering. But without Alicia, there was no way I could stick around. I swerved, made a big U turn, and headed home.

I rode back up McClellan Street, turned right on Thirty-fourth Street, and pedaled as fast as I could up to my house.

"Yoo-hoo, Jane!"

Oh, no. It was Needlehead, waving to me like mad from her yard.

23

"I'm in a hurry, Dr. Need — uh — I mean, Dr. Heedlemaker." I'd been afraid of that. Alicia and I had called her Needlehead so often I almost forgot her real name.

"It will merely take a minute, Jane!" she called over her fence.

Yuk! I was trapped. What if she wanted to experiment on me or something? I got off my bike in front of her gate. "It's urgent that I return home immediately," I told her, getting right back on my bike.

"If you're not interested in earning some money next week, Jane, I can ask your brother."

"Money?"

"Yes. Fifty cents a day for a week. I'm going to a conference and I need someone to water my plants."

"Watering your plants?" That sounded easy enough for three-fifty. "That's all?"

"That's all that's required. I'll indicate what each plant needs before I leave."

"You got a deal. Thanks." I jumped back on my bike. Putting up with Needlehead's plants should be a snap, I thought as I parked my bike in the garage and went upstairs.

But when I got to my room, I wondered — what if this was another research project in disguise? Maybe she'd have hidden video cameras all over her house, observing the plant-watering behavior of seventh-grade girls. I worried about this a little, but finally decided that even though Needlehead was weird — she wasn't sneaky.

But the thought of the seventh grade got me wondering about just how people *are* supposed to act in junior high. I got scared all over again knowing I was going there with no friends.

24

Suddenly, I had an idea. Why couldn't I do research like Dr. Needlehead does? When school started, I could observe everyone the way she observed me to see who the popular people are and to figure out what they do to be popular. Then all I'd have to do is copy them! I fished around my desk looking for a notebook like the one Dr. Needlehead had used when she followed me around. I couldn't find anything like that, so I used the back of a piece of wrapping paper. On the top of it I wrote:

THE JANE G. HIGGINS POPULARITY PROJECT

It's strange, but right after I wrote the word "popularity," I felt guilty — as though I were doing something wrong. I folded up the paper and put it in my desk. I didn't have to think about it very long before I knew exactly why I had the guilt attack. My mom has a very strong opinion about kids wanting to be popular. Mom thinks it's one of the great mistakes in life. She says that the people who really amount to something in this world were never the popular people when they were kids. Then she makes this speech: "Take Orville Redenbacher. He went to my high school, everyone thought he was a nerd, and now look at him — he's the popcorn king of the United States." Mom also says that if she hadn't been so worried about being popular in high school and trying to get boys to like her, maybe she would have gone to medical school. I shut my desk drawer. I knew I wasn't going to get any help from her as far my popularity project went. In fact, I didn't even want to tell her about it.

Down the hall, I could hear Mom talking to Gramps in his room. She probably didn't know I had come back from the park. The door was open, and I couldn't help hearing everything she said.

25

"Dad, we need your help. We've been so worried about Jane — her friend Alicia left today for California, and Janie's terribly upset. We thought if you would take her to Seattle Center Saturday, it would help to get her feeling good again — the rest of us can't go. We have to go to John's first soccer game. How 'bout it, Dad? Will you do that for Janie?"

I held my breath, wondering what would Gramps say. Then I heard him.

"Buszhburmph mershrum."

Three

Saturday I was in my room discussing my life with Juliet; it seemed like she was the only one I talked to since Alicia moved. I was telling her that Mom said Gramps was going to take me to Seattle Center but that I still didn't believe he really would. I was also telling her how much I missed Alicia, imagining Juliet might even understand, since she had seemed very unhappy a few years ago when our cat, Romeo, died. But Juliet pulled away and tore downstairs, barking and barking. She was going nuts. I knew that could only mean one thing — the mailman. I galloped down the stairs, two at a time. Maybe I'd have a letter from Alicia!

I tried to block Juliet from going out, but she leaped between my legs.

"Juliet! Come back here!" I commanded.

I might as well have been shouting "good doggie." I get no respect from Juliet if the mailman is in the picture. She hates him. She charged toward him, totally ignoring me, barking and growling even more.

"Juliet. Stop that!" I ordered, wasting my breath once again.

Luckily the gate was closed, but she stuck her face through the slats, trying to take little bites out of his leg while he was putting the mail in the box. It's a good thing her nose isn't two inches longer, or his leg would be dog food.

The mailman shook his fist at me. "I'm mad as hell, and I'm not going to take it anymore!"

I didn't know what to say. His face had turned purple.

"That damn dog!"

"She can't get out — uh — you're really very safe." But Juliet was barking so loud, I wasn't sure he heard me.

"You tell your parents to move that mailbox away from that animal or I'll just skip your house!" He stuffed the mail in our box and stomped down the street. The back of his neck was still bright red.

"Juliet, you need a little refresher course at obedience school," I muttered as I grabbed her collar and dragged her toward the house. I was dying to get the mail but with her enemy, the mailman, still on the block, I didn't dare open the gate until I had gotten her locked inside. Could he really skip our house? That would be terrible.

When I pulled out the mail, right on top — was a letter from Alicia! She's into stickers a lot, and she had some nice ones, all rainbows and hearts, plastered all over the envelope. I looked at the San Jose postmark. Poor Alicia, I thought, not even living in her own house and in a place where they have earthquakes — she must be as miserable as I am. I raced up to my room to read it, with Juliet bounding after me. I flopped down on the bed, and Juliet did too, so I had to go shut the door in case Mom was around. I tore open the letter.

Dear Janie,

California is so-o-o-o-o-o great! My cousin, Kelly, isn't a nerd at all! She's really great and just my age! We went to the beach yesterday. My aunt drove us there. The beaches are in this place called Santa Cruz. We went to one called Natural Bridges State Beach. My cousin knew these two guys who go to the same school I'm going to go to. They kept walking by us on and off all afternoon. Sometimes they'd say hi and then they'd run and jump on each other and start throwing sand at each other. I think she likes one of them, named Curt, but I thought the other one was better looking. His name was Derek. I can't wait for school to start here. Say hi to everybody for me! Don't do anything I wouldn't do — HA! HA!

LOVE AND HUGS,
Alicia

P.S. Did you know that when Prince Edward quit the military, he didn't know what to do with his life, because the royal people aren't allowed to be doctors or lawyers or anything like that? I think he should be a rock star. He could call himself PRINCE!!

I put the letter down and just sat there for a few minutes. I couldn't believe that after being there just one day, Alicia seemed so happy — she was even meeting guys! My biggest date was going to Seattle Center with my grandfather.

I knew I should be happy for Alicia. I really tried to be, but it didn't work. I read the letter a couple of more times, then I put my arms around Juliet. When she licked my face, I was crying.

I felt terrible about being upset. People are supposed to be happy when nice things happen for their friends. I couldn't even laugh at her joke about Prince Edward. Alicia was always funny — she has a great personality. Everyone in our class looked up to her. Alicia was the great Alicia Haglund, star forward on the Mt. Baker Bombers girl soccer team, Alicia Haglund, star of *Wind in the Willows*, the sixth-grade play. I was Jane what's-her-name, Alicia's friend. That truly was my entire claim to fame in both the fifth grade and the sixth grade at Evergreen Elementary. Alicia was the one who made things go; she had all the ideas about how to be and what to do; my talent was following. I knew now that glomming on to just one good friend had been a big mistake for me but not for Alicia. All she would have to do is be her spectacular self and people would appear like magic, following her around, wanting to be her new friends. At Martin Luther King, Jr., Junior High without Alicia Haglund, I'd be invisible — people probably wouldn't even know I went there.

I lay there, holding on to Juliet, getting a large dose of dog germs from her many kisses. Now that I'd gotten a letter from Alicia, I'd *have* to write back. I made myself get out my stationery, and even though I was sniffling after every sentence I wrote, I tried to sound cheerful.

Dear Alicia,
Hi! California sounds so great! I loved your
letter! Did you go surfing at the beach? Is
Hollywood nearby? After you left, when I got back
from the airport, I was riding my bike in the
park, and you'll never guess who I saw, of all
people — Darrell Williams and Brian Kimura
and guess what?!! They looked so cute!! I couldn't

believe it! Not all rumply and scuzzy like they did
last year. When they saw me, they yelled for me to
play tennis with them. Darrell had an extra
racket. It was so fun. Every time I missed a shot
he said, "Nice try, Janie." Wasn't that great of
him? How are things in your new neighborhood?
It's great your cousin is not a nerd. Well, I guess
that's about it. Don't do anything I wouldn't
do — HA! HA!

> *Love,*
> *Janie xxx ooo*

P.S. I miss you a lot.

As I put the letter in the envelope, I couldn't quite
believe what I had written. I don't know what happened,
but my pen just seemed to take off by itself. I read the
letter over. I knew I should cross out that stuff about
playing tennis with Darrell and Brian, but it was so nice
reading about it.

As I licked the envelope, Mom called up to me.

"Jane!"

"What?"

"Are you ready? Gramps is waiting for you!"

I had been so upset about Alicia's letter that I had
totally forgotten that Gramps and I were supposed to
leave for Seattle Center at one o'clock. Juliet jumped off
my bed while I got up and went to the top of the stairs
and called down to Mom.

"I'll be ready in just a minute."

"Well, hurry up, honey. You should leave in five minutes, if you want to make the bus for downtown. Gramps
can't run like you can, you know."

"Okay. I'll hurry." I went to the bathroom and
splashed cold water on my face and brushed my hair. I

hoped it didn't look as if I had been crying. Mom can almost always tell; I was afraid she would try to get me to talk about it. When I heard her ask Gramps to take me to Seattle Center because they were worried about me since Alicia left, I thought it was a little trick Mom was using to get Gramps out of the house. But as I looked in the mirror at my puffy eyes, I was starting to wonder. I ran down the stairs. Gramps was waiting for me by the front door.

"All set, Gramps?" I looked up at him, hoping I looked as enthusiastic as I was trying to sound.

"Mstrburmp," Gramps mumbled, and nodded. Just like I thought, no teeth. But we were actually getting him out of the house. At least that was progress!

"Have fun, you two." Mom kissed us both good-bye, and we headed down the street to the bus stop.

I looked at my watch. At the rate we were going, I was sure we'd never make the bus. Gramps walks really slow; he sort of shuffles along. I looked over at him. He was wearing these gray baggy pants and a gray sweater and a brownish gray raincoat. Almost everything about him seemed gray. He's bald, with a little fringe of white hair around his head, and his eyes seemed gray and watery. These days even his skin seemed kind of gray.

We walked by the park, and I looked around casually to see if anyone I knew was there. A bunch of high school guys were playing touch football. But when I looked over in the corner of the park and spotted the group in the little kids' playground, I wanted to die. It was Darrell Williams and Brian Kimura with none other than Rhonda Whipple and Nalita Jones, the two girls from our sixth-grade class that all the boys went bonkers over, saying that Rhonda looked like Madonna and Nalita looked like Whitney Houston. The stupid boys would practically drool on those girls. Rhonda and Nalita sat on the swings, laughing their heads off, while Brian and Darrell hung upside down from the top of the jungle gym, waving their arms around. They were having a great time. The last thing I wanted was for them to see me shuffling along with Gramps! I scooted around the other side of him, hoping he'd block me from sight. I wanted to help Gramps more than anything but not with the whole school watching. When we got to the bus stop and sat down, I grabbed a newspaper someone had left and hid behind it. But every once in a while, I couldn't help taking a peek around the side of the paper. They were having so much fun. If I had been with Alicia instead of Gramps, I knew she would have yelled to them and we would have run right over there.

Pretty soon the bus came. I got on behind Gramps, still holding the newspaper in front of my face. We got a seat near the middle door. I sat on the inside, near the window, and Gramps sat next to me. As the bus pulled away on McClellan, I peered around the paper. Darrell and Brian were still hanging upside down, but now Rhonda and Nalita were jumping all around them, trying to tickle them. When the girls got too close, Brian and Darrel would try to grab them.

The bus headed down McClellan, stopped at the light, and then turned on Rainier. I couldn't stop thinking about the fun those kids were having and wishing Alicia were here so maybe we could be in the middle of some fun stuff like that. I sure wouldn't mind if those boys tried to grab me. Unfortunately, these thoughts were suddenly interrupted.

"Huggrurhmmmmmmmm."

"What?" I looked over at Gramps, but his eyes were closed and his hands were folded across his chest. He was snoring. I glanced around, hoping no one noticed.

"Huggrurhmmmmmmmm." Gramps snored again, louder this time. It was embarrassing. At least there wasn't anyone on the bus I knew.

He snored all the way downtown. As the bus got close to Third Avenue, where we were supposed to get off, I gently put my hand on Gramps's arm and tried to wake him up.

"Gramps — wake up. We're almost here."

"Hrmmrup."

I shook his arm a little bit, and slowly he opened his eyes. As he looked around he seemed so confused that I got worried.

"We have to get off the bus in a minute."

Gramps nodded but he still looked mixed up.

"You're taking me to Seattle Center," I whispered, "so I can have fun there."

He sat up a little straighter, took off his glasses, and rubbed his eyes. When the bus came to a stop he put on his glasses, got up, and headed right for the door. Thank goodness, he was okay. He even seemed to shuffle less after his nap. I left my seat, taking the newspaper with me — you never know who you might run into. As I climbed down the steps, I looked at Gramps. There he was, standing right in the middle of downtown — the first time in months! I went over to him and gave his hand a squeeze.

On the way to Westlake Mall to get the monorail for Seattle Center, we walked by all the stores. Red and gold leaves hung from Nordstrom's display windows, and all the mannequins were dressed in beautiful red clothes. I wished I knew what to wear the first day of school. Mom took me shopping last week, and I got some jeans and two sweaters, a red one and a purple one. If I could have gone with Alicia instead of Mom, or if I could have waited until school started to see what the other people had on, I would have felt a lot more confident about what I picked out. It was bad enough to have to show up on the first day with no friends, but if your clothes were dumb, too, it would be ten times worse.

Gramps and I climbed the steps up to the place where you get on the monorail. Right underneath us a steel-drum band was playing; it was great. I love downtown.

We lucked out, because as soon as we got to the top of the stairs, the monorail pulled up.

"How do you like the band, Gramps?" I asked when we were in our seats.

"Phrrryguh." Gramps smiled and nodded. It sounded like what he said was "pretty good."

Gramps seemed to be perking up. That was the first time I'd seen him smile in a long time. I was afraid to get my hopes up too much, but I couldn't help getting excited. Maybe Mom's plan really would work!

Seattle Center was jumping with people; it's always like that when it's a beautiful day. I was looking around when swoooosh! A guy whizzed by on a skateboard. He was wearing a Bon Jovi T-shirt and looked around thirteen; he had brown hair. I wanted to really check him out, casually of course, but he had zoomed by too fast. I couldn't see much else. He pivoted to a stop in front of the Center House and waited there with one foot on the skateboard. I wondered if he had a bunch of friends who would show up, but pretty soon an old lady in a green dress came up to him. He put his skateboard under his arm and they went in the Center House together. Mom was right, there were people of all ages here.

Gramps and I wandered by the fountains. There were lots of street musicians and mimes around — even though a zillion songs jumbled in the air, to me it all sounded wonderful. Everywhere people lay on the grass. I noticed a lot of them were eating.

"How about getting some food, Gramps?"

Gramps smiled and nodded, so we strolled over to the Center House; it's a building that has all kinds of food stands lining the walls and a fountain in the middle. There's a second level with souvenir and craft shops, but the whole thing is open, not like a regular two-story place. When we got inside, we could hear a different band playing — it was old-fashioned music, definitely not Top Forty material. We walked over to the food stalls; Gramps bought me a huge soft pretzel and got an Orange Julius for himself.

"Want to go upstairs where the music's coming from?" I asked, chomping on my pretzel.

Gramps smiled again and headed right up the stairs. I followed him, and when I got up there, I saw an amazing sight. Men and women were dancing all around, holding each other in their arms, swaying to the music; some were shuffling around the dance floor, others were sliding, gliding, and swooping. I couldn't believe it. Every single couple looked at least eighty years old!

Gramps and I stood watching them. I finished eating my pretzel and peeked at Gramps, but he hadn't even taken a sip of his Orange Julius. He just stared.

Finally, he bent down and whispered to me, with his hand covering his mouth. "Wnnsridwn?"

I wasn't sure what he meant until he pointed to the tables next to the dance floor.

"Sure. Let's sit down."

We found an empty table close to the band and sat down. Gramps didn't move a muscle; he just sat, his eyes glued to the dance floor. Finally, he began to sip his Orange Julius. Then the table started to wiggle, and when I looked underneath, I saw his foot tapping against the base.

The band was pretty corny, I thought. All the men had on light blue jackets, except for one bald guy in a sparkly red one, playing a trumpet. Behind them on a curtain was a banner that said: JERRY SWEENEY AND THE SWEETNOTES. Not a single Sweetnote seemed under seventy, but they were very energetic. The bald one in the red jacket was especially lively, snapping his fingers as he led the band. Jerry Sweeney, no doubt. I was looking around when across the room I spotted someone else snapping his fingers; he was definitely under seventy. It was the same boy I had seen with the skateboard; he had it propped up against the table where he was sitting. Now that he wasn't zooming by on it, I could get a good look at him. I didn't want to stare, so I casually looked at him, then at Jerry Sweeney, then back at him. He wasn't gorgeous or anything, like River Phoenix, but he wouldn't win an ugly contest either. Kind of plain, like me, I guess. Why would a guy wearing a Bon Jovi T-shirt be snapping his fingers to Jerry Sweeney and the Sweetnotes? But then I saw that he had earphones on and was listening to a Walkman. Even after the Sweetnotes had stopped playing, he kept snapping his fingers. Then that same lady in the green dress I had seen him with outside left the dance floor and went to sit next to him. I wondered who they were.

Pretty soon the music started up again. Gramps and I stayed where we were, just watching. Gramps was watching the people dancing, and I was watching the guy with the skateboard. When I thought I might get caught staring, I looked at the dance floor, and I began to realize that even though the Sweetnotes were totally corny, this

37

dance wasn't so dumb. Many of the ladies had on pretty dresses, and a lot of the men had on suits; some of the couples even twirled around, and a few of them did fancy steps. Even the people taking a time-out on the sidelines looked like they couldn't wait to get back on the dance floor. If only I could get Gramps out there — these people were having so much fun!

"Gramps, why don't you ask someone to dance?"

Gramps shook his head.

"There seem to be a lot of nice ladies sitting around, Gramps, why don't you?" I gestured to the right of us, where there were three tables all filled with ladies.

Gramps turned away as if he hadn't heard me.

I started counting the ladies to convince him how many there were. "Gramps — I've counted nine just in this part of the room!"

He shook his head again; he seemed very upset.

"Nine of 'em right under your nose. There are zillions more ladies than men in this place. It's a man's paradise!"

"Nnsnwld dncwwimme," he blurted out.

"Gramps, I can't understand what you said."

Gramps looked away. He had stopped tapping his foot and he seemed sad, and shaky, too, like he was nervous. He took a pen from his shirt pocket, and the bus schedule. Then he wrote on the back of the schedule what he had tried to tell me. Gramps's writing is kind of wiggly and scribbly, but I could read it. The note said:

No one would want to dance with me.

Four

The monorail sped away from Seattle Center and headed downtown. Gramps slumped in the seat next to me. He wasn't sleeping, he was just staring down at the floor.

"Gramps, I know those ladies would dance with you — and, well — I'm sure, I mean — if you wore your teeth then they'd be able to understand you when you asked them to dance."

Gramps didn't even seem to hear me.

"They'd understand everything — anything you might want to talk about. You could have some nice conversations with those ladies while you were dancing."

Gramps turned his face away from me and took his handkerchief out of his pocket and blew his nose.

"You could talk about the Minnesota Vikings. You know everything there is to know about them, or if the lady didn't like football — maybe bird-watching. Mom said you can recognize a ton of birds. That would make interesting conversation." I looked out the window of the monorail down on the roofs of the buildings below.

Finally, I decided to shut up. I was probably just making things worse.

When we got home, Mom practically pounced on us the minute she heard the door open.

"Well, you two — how'd it go? Did you have fun?"

"Well, uh — there sure were a lot of people there. How was John's soccer game?" I asked quickly. Any more talk about Seattle Center would probably just make Gramps feel worse.

"They lost," Mom answered, then zeroed right in again. "What about you, Dad? Did you have fun?"

"Hrrmph." Gramps mumbled and shuffled up the stairs to his room. We heard him shut the door hard.

"Janie, what happened? Gramps seems upset."

"I know. I think he is."

"Come on in the kitchen while I get a cup of coffee, and tell me all about it."

I sat down at the kitchen table across from Mom and explained how things had gone pretty well until the dance. Then I reached in my pocket and took the bus schedule Gramps had written on and handed it to her.

Mom was quiet for a few minutes. Finally she said, "Gramps and my mother loved to dance. They went to dances at the Optimist Club in St. Paul practically right up until the time Gramma died." Mom held her coffee cup in both hands and didn't say anything for the longest time. When she finally looked up, there were tears in her eyes.

"He must think he can never have any fun without her." The second I said that, I remembered seeing Alicia walk onto that plane, and I got a lump in my throat.

"He must miss Gramma so much." I kept swallowing, trying to make the lump go away.

"I was very lucky, Janie, compared to a lot of people

I know. I had parents who stayed very much in love. Remember how Gramps used to call Gramma 'my bride'? I think he always thought of her that way. It really was 'till death do us part.' "

"You mean like what they say in weddings."

Mom nodded.

"Mom, there were zillions of nice old ladies at that dance. I'm sure they have no husbands and would love to dance with Gramps. If we could just get him to believe that!"

Mom sat there not saying anything. Then, all of a sudden, she jumped up from the table. "I'm going to call Seattle Center right now and find out when the next seniors dance is!" She grabbed the phone book from the counter, looked up the number, and then called. I waited while Mom scribbled on the pad by the phone and talked to them in her nurse voice, which is very businesslike.

"Janie — they have them all the time!"

"Really?"

"You bet. Every Wednesday, Friday, and Saturday from one to three in the afternoon until Labor Day, then every Saturday night from eight to eleven."

"But how are we going to get him there? I mean, if it just reminds him of all the fun he had with Gramma and makes him miss her and get sad, I don't see how we can get him to go."

"He'll do it for you. You've just got to ask him and think of some reason to tell him why you want to go to Seattle Center again. Think about it, okay?"

"Well, okay."

"Remember the Skagit!"

I laughed. It was funny about the Skagit. I knew exactly what Mom meant.

We used to have the best time when Gramps and

Gramma visited us from St. Paul. My grandparents were both members of the Sierra Club. They loved going hiking, and especially bird watching. If it had to do with nature, Gramps was crazy about it; he had the world's largest collection of *National Geographics*. (I used to love to read them. Actually, I liked to look at the pictures of the naked people. I always felt a little bit weird about this. One time I talked to Mom about it. I told her I liked to look at the naked people — even the ladies — and I asked her if that was weird. Mom is really something about stuff like that. My mom can talk about bodies the way most people can talk about the weather. Probably that's because she's a nurse. She just said, "Why, of course you like to look at those pictures. The human body is just wonderful. And when you don't see it without clothes on very often, it makes it quite exciting when you do. And breasts are just like pizza." I thought this was crazy, and I asked Mom what she meant. She said, "Everyone likes pizza. Everyone likes breasts. They're the very first things that fed us all, for heaven's sakes, so they always seem quite wonderful. Like pizza." I don't know what it is about my Mom, but she just makes you feel better about stuff like that.)

Anyway, once we were at the Seattle aquarium when Gramps and Gramma were in town, and I noticed a stack of pamphlets by a sign that said EAGLE WATCH. I always go for free handouts, so I grabbed one. It said biologists from the aquarium were taking people on Skagit River raft trips to see bald eagles. "Hey, everybody," I said, "This would be some serious bird watching!" They thought it was a dumb idea. This trip was in January. It's wet, cold, and gray in January in Seattle, and you'd have to be very interested in bald eagles to want to do this. I thought it would be a great adventure. I talked about it so much, I think Gramps finally said he'd take me just to shut me up. Gramps and I had a super time on that Skagit trip, even though it rained and rained, and we only saw one bald eagle. I was thrilled when I saw that bird, although the man next to me insisted it was a crow. When we hit a little white water, I huddled in the raft next to Gramps, and when he started singing "Singin' in the Rain," I sang, too. The man who said my eagle was a crow said, "Spare me," through chattering teeth, while everyone else stared at us and shivered. But pretty soon it rained even harder, and they finally all gave in and started singing, too. Gramps got that whole group jamming! Ever since then, Mom's been convinced I can get Gramps to go anywhere.

But getting Gramps to go down the Skagit River in January seemed like a piece of cake, compared to getting him to go back to that dance. I couldn't imagine what I was supposed to act so interested in that would make it seem like I just couldn't wait to get back there. It certainly wasn't Jerry Sweeney and the Sweetnotes.

Then it hit me! All of a sudden, I had a great plan. I got a piece of my stationery from my desk, and I wrote Gramps this note:

Dear Gramps,
Thank you very much for taking me to Seattle
Center. I had a good time, even if you didn't.
Would it be too much trouble for you to take me
again? Don't tell Mom (or anyone) but I want to
see if the boy with the skateboard comes there all
the time. Mom found out they have those seniors
dances on Saturday night, starting next week. I
don't want anyone to know the real reason I want
to go back there. It would be embarrassing. Could

we pretend I want to go to the Science Center?
They have a dinosaur exhibit there now. How
'bout it?

Love xxx oooo,
Janie

I went down the hall to Gramps's room. I wasn't sure if he was awake, even though I heard the TV on in his room, because he falls asleep in front of it a lot. So I just slipped the note under his door.

Just then Juliet escaped from John's room, with the flag hanging from her tail.

"She got to 'what so proudly we hail!' " he announced triumphantly as he dove after her. The flag flopped off as Juliet bounded down the steps. John just doesn't know when to give up.

"JANE! JOHN! Dinner's ready — tell Gramps — it's time to eat."

Gramps came out of his room, so I knew he had heard Mom yelling for us to come to dinner. John charged down the stairs, three at a time, and I went after him and Gramps followed me. I wondered if he had read the note, but I decided not to mention it. I didn't want to bug him.

"Where's Dad?" I asked Mom. He always makes dinner with Mom, but I hadn't heard him come home, and he wasn't in the kitchen.

"He called and said he'd be late at the office. He told us to go ahead without him."

"Oh boy! Pasgetti!" John looked in the pot on the stove. He used to call it that when he was four, and now everyone except me calls it that. How corny.

Mom whooshed the spaghetti off the stove and dumped it into a bowl. She held her head away from it

44

while she handed it to me to put on the table. I guess she didn't want to smell it too much and get tempted. "John, get the salad out of the refrigerator," she said solemnly as she cut a lemon.

Gramps sat down and John and I put the food on the table. Mom looked at the spaghetti longingly while we heaped it on our plates. Then she took a deep breath and clobbered the lemon, squeezing it as hard as she could all over her salad. She picked at the lettuce, just taking a few bites and chewing in slow motion while the rest of us scarfed down the spaghetti. When we were about halfway through dinner, Dad came home.

"Oh boy, pasgetti!" Dad smiled.

I just rolled my eyes.

"How is everyone?" He put his briefcase down and then came over to the table and kissed Mom. "Let me wash up and I'll be right there." When he got back to the table, he asked everyone how their day was while he warmed up some spaghetti in the microwave.

"Okay." John slurped up the last of his spaghetti. He had a slimy red mustache and beard, and noodles stuck on his nose. It was slob city at his end of the table.

"John, don't talk with your mouth full," Mom said. She has a big thing about that.

"Well, he asked, didn't he?"

"Janie? What'd you do today?"

I pointed to my mouth — I couldn't answer.

"We went to Seattle Center."

The whole family stared. The words had come from Gramps.

"We're going back soon —" Gramps cleared his throat, "to a dinosaur exhibit."

I couldn't believe it. No one could . . . Gramps was wearing his teeth.

Five

Sometimes in life the things you worry about never turn out to be quite as bad as you think they'll be, but my first week of school wasn't like that. It completely measured up to all my horrible expectations.

To begin with, I was clueless about what to wear, even though I had been worrying about it all summer. The night before school started, after I came back from watering Needlehead's plants, I tried on every outfit I had. Every blouse I owned looked little-girly, like it had sixth grade written all over it. I bet I changed my clothes a hundred times. Pants and blouses were flying everywhere until I finally ended up plopped down in the middle of my room with my clothes heaped all over like a rummage sale. Juliet walked around, stepping on my clothes, getting her hair all over everything. At that point I didn't even care that I'd be starting the seventh grade dressed in dog hair.

That night I missed Alicia more than ever. I dug out the lipstick she'd given me from my underwear drawer, put a little on, and stared in the mirror. Was it too much?

Did I look ridiculous? I just couldn't take the chance that it might look totally silly, so I wiped it off.

If only Alicia had been here — it would have been so great experimenting. One of my favorite things about Alicia is how she makes everything fun. Her mother would have helped, too. Alicia's mother has a big weight problem, but she's really pretty. She's a model at Dede's Queen Boutique, which is a large-lady clothes store. She had all the latest makeup and hair stuff. Trying on her makeup was fabulous — it saved money, too. It's impossible to figure out what makeup to buy without spending a year's worth of babysitting money.

One time I spent hours studying the lipstick chart at Pay 'n Save, narrowed it down to either Poppysilk Red or Brandied Snow Peach and finally blew all my money, practically six dollars, on Brandied Snow Peach. I couldn't wait to have lovely peachy lips. When I got home I stood in front of my mirror, carefully stroked it over my lips, and watched my mouth turn moldy green. My brother (who thinks he's a comedian but is not funny) stared at me and then galloped through the house, screaming that the place was haunted.

I finally decided to play it safe as far as my clothes went and just wear jeans, my Adidas, and my favorite short-sleeved red cotton sweater. I washed my hair, tried to make it do more than just hang there, gave up in disgust, and finally went to bed. I let Juliet sleep with me, so I didn't feel so friendless.

We never have breakfast together at our house because we all have to leave at different times. Mom goes to the hospital at seven-fifteen. Dad is usually eating Raisin Bran when I get downstairs, then he leaves at seven forty-five. John leaves last because he doesn't have to be at Evergreen Elementary until nine. He practically gets up one second before he has to leave, too. Sometimes I think that kid doesn't even brush his teeth.

That morning I was sitting at the breakfast table, eating my Frosted Flakes, when Gramps came down. He put some bread in the toaster and then sat across from me at the table. "Mornin'."

"Hi, Gramps." It was weird being able to understand Gramps again. I hadn't realized how much I had gotten used to him mumbling without his teeth. But Gramps still wasn't back to normal. Since Gramma died he hasn't talked nearly as much as he used to, but, at least, now I could understand him.

"Today's the first day of school —" I reached for my milk glass, and just then it just slid out of my hand. "Oh, no!" It spilled all over the table — and all over my jeans!

"Tch, tch."

"Gramps!" I looked at my watch. "I have to get to the bus — I don't have time to change!"

"Mustn't cry —"

"What? I'm not crying — I —"

"Over spilt milk."

"Oh, Gramps! I'm a mess!"

"Run."

"What?"

"Run. Air'll dry it."

I jumped up and got some paper towels and tried to dry it off. "Oh, Gramps. I can't be late."

"You have lunch money?" Gramps walked me to the door.

I nodded. "Mom gave it to me last night."

Gramps bent down and kissed me on the cheek.

"Will running really work, Gramps?"

"Don't worry. It'll dry."

I went out the back door and ran as fast as I could for the bus stop. I couldn't believe it. Here I spent all last night trying to figure out about clothes and makeup and I end up starting junior high looking like I wet my pants!

At the bus stop there were some kids from my sixth-grade class hanging around. It was the popular people — the same ones I had seen in the park the other day — Rhonda Whipple, Nalita Jones, Darrell Williams, and Brian Kimura. They were laughing and talking. They didn't say a word to me when I got to the bus stop. It's true, I thought; without Alicia, I am no one. I stood around in my wet pants, looking at the trees in the park, pretending not to care that no one acted like I was there. Then the bus came, and they all bunched up and climbed on. I followed, straggling after them. Nalita Jones kind of mumbled, "Hi," to me over her shoulder because I was right behind her. Then she ran to the back of the bus and sat with the rest of them. You always know when people don't want you to join in. They don't even have to tell you to go away. You just know that they don't want you.

I sat by myself in the middle of the bus. At least no one was close enough to see my stupid jeans. They were finally starting to dry, but you could still see that something had spilled on them. When we got to King Junior High, I was one of the last to get off. The school looked gigantic! All I could think of was how cozy everything had been in the sixth grade. Who would have thought I'd miss old Evergreen Elementary? But here I was wishing I'd gone there with John today. I wouldn't even have minded if he called me a blooey grunt.

As soon as I got inside the front doors, I took the map they had sent us out of my pocket. I tried to figure out where room 333 was; it was supposed to be my home-room. While I was staring at the map a tall, pretty girl came up to me.

"Can I help you find your homeroom?"

"Thanks!" I held out the map and looked up at her gratefully. *Wow*. She looked like someone who should be on MTV. I felt like a midget in this place — the eighth- and ninth-graders were as gigantic as the school. She had on a Cub Guide badge, so I knew she was an official type of person, probably a ninth-grader. The mascot of King Junior High is a lion, and the seventh graders are called cubs.

"You need to go to the stairs at the end of this hall," she said, pointing to her left with beautiful long, red fingernails. "Then go up to the third floor, and it's in the middle of the hall on the right side."

"Thanks a lot!" I smiled and headed for the stairs. I can't tell you how good it was to have someone talk to me — even if it was her job.

As I walked up the stairs to the third floor, I thought about my homeroom. I was hoping that the homeroom teacher would have assigned seats. Then it's not so obvious if you don't have anyone to sit with. I lucked out. When I got to room 333, Mr. Chung, the teacher, was reading off the names and assigning seats. I recognized a few people from Evergreen Elementary, but no one said hi or anything; people were too busy finding their seats. I ended up sitting between a boy named Seth Hifler and a girl named Stacey Hiraki. I don't know what elementary school they went to, but they weren't from Evergreen.

The classes weren't bad as far as not having any friends was concerned — everyone's so busy trying to listen on the first day and there are so many people from different elementary schools that no one really knows each other. But lunch was terrible. It was even worse than the bus. Out of all my classes, Yolanda Johnson was the one person I talked to from Evergreen, and she had a different lunch period than I did. I ended up eating alone, sitting at the end of a lunch table by myself while a bunch of eighth- or ninth-grade girls had a great time, showing each other their schedules, talking and laughing together at the other end. They had beautiful makeup and cool hairstyles; our table must have looked like a bunch of models from *Seventeen* with one midget on the end: me.

The bus ride home after school was even more awful than it had been in the morning. Bouncing along at seven-thirty A.M., I had hope I might find a friendly person during the day. At three-thirty P.M., I sat with the exact same number of friends as when I started — zero. My worst fears had come true.

As soon as I got home, I leafed through the mail. There was nothing from Alicia. She must have been having too great a time to write me. Just to be sure, I checked all the letters twice. Then I checked them again . . . nothing.

The first week is always short, since school starts on the Tuesday after Labor Day, but it seemed like a century. Wednesday, Thursday, and Friday were just as bad as the first day had been. Gramps was up in his room watching TV when I got home on Friday, and the whole terrible week was finally over.

I stuck my head in his door. "Can I come in?"

"Mmm-hmm." Gramps nodded and motioned me in.

I was glad he was awake. I plopped down on the floor in front of the TV, next to where he sat in his rocking chair. I thought just being in there with him would make me feel better, but when I looked up at him everything came pouring out.

"I had a terrible week, Gramps! There was no one to talk to on the bus, and at lunch I sat alone. I don't have any idea how to get to know anybody! What do you think I should do?"

"Grspmepsioo hrmprrrsn."

"Oh, Gramps — you stopped wearing your teeth again." I looked over at his dresser. The teeth were just sitting there in the glass. If Gramps went back to Seattle Center with no teeth, it wouldn't work at all. I sat there feeling hopeless about both of us. When I started to feel like I was about to cry, I got up to leave.

Gramps waved his arms around and pointed to his mouth — I guess he didn't want me to leave. I didn't know what he was trying to tell me, so I waited while he went over to his dresser and put his teeth in.

After he got them in, he moved his mouth around funny for a minute. Then he said, "I forgot."

"Oh."

"Say hi."

"Huh?"

"Say hi to people."

"You mean to make friends?"

Gramps nodded.

"You mean to people I don't know?"

Gramps nodded again. "They don't come down the chimney."

"What?"

"Friends don't come down the chimney."

"Oh." I couldn't tell if Gramps was really trying to tell me something or if he was kind of confused, the way he gets sometimes when he first wakes up.

I went to my room. I lay on the floor and stared at the ceiling and thought about what Gramps had said. I knew he was trying, but what kind of advice was that — telling me to say hi to people and that friends don't come down the chimney? If Gramps had been his old self, I bet he would have given me some real advice.

School had been such a disaster that I realized I hadn't been calm enough to even think about my popularity plan. In fact, I had completely forgotten it. I went to my desk and got the piece of paper with "THE JANE G. HIGGINS POPULARITY PROJECT" written on it. I stared at the blank page. Some project — by the time I even figured out who the popular people were, everyone would probably be set in their little groups. Everyone except me. How *was* I going to make friends? I sat there, staring at the notebook.

If only things were different. I could just see it. ZAM! Monday morning, by magic, I would go to school and as I walked through the halls, dozens of people would say hi to me; everyone would know me — just like my brother, I'd have more friends than a dog has fleas. Wow! It would be so great. Friends, friends, everywhere I looked. "Hi, Janie!" "Hey, Janie — wait up!" "Janie — come here a second!" They'd all be calling my name. Even ninth-graders — even guys! It would be so wonderful! I sat there enjoying this idea very much and then, all of a sudden, it hit me. Gramps *was* right. Friends don't come down the chimney. . . . They don't just show up in your life like magic. *You do have to do something.* I would have to do something to make friends.

I sat there and thought about this. What should I do? Where do you start, anyway? Then I thought some more about what Gramps said. Where else do you start if you don't start with saying hi? It had sounded like pretty weak advice — but he really could be right. So I took my pen and, under the heading "THE JANE G. HIG-GINS POPULARITY PROJECT," I wrote:

1. Say hi to everyone.

I imagined myself going down the halls of King Junior High, saying, "Hi . . . Hi . . . Hi . . . Hi . . . Hi," to every single person. That would be a little too weird, I decided. I crossed it out and changed it to:

1. Say hi to every third person

That was more reasonable. But then I thought of another problem. I went to Gramps's room and knocked on the door.

"Gramps, can I come in again?"

"Yep."

"What if I do say hi to people I don't know, and they ask me how I know them?"

"Lie." Gramps winked.

"What?" I didn't think I had heard him right.

"Make it up."

"Oh." I stood there thinking about this while Gramps watched "Hollywood Squares." "Could I say something like, I thought I knew them from summer camp?"

Gramps nodded.

"Okay, thanks." I went back to my room, shut the door and looked in the mirror. "Oh, didn't you go to Hidden Valley Camp?" I said casually. Then I tried, "I thought I knew you from Hidden Valley Camp," and "Weren't you in girls' tent four? I was in three." I decided I really should give this a try. The thought of another week like this was horrible. Anything would be better, and, besides, it didn't seem as if I had much to lose. Then I wondered, if it did work, what if I made all nerd friends? My group might be a gathering of nerds. I thought about this a minute but then decided that I had to face the fact that I was probably one anyway without Alicia.

I looked over the plan. I hoped I really would be brave enough to try it on Monday, but at least I had the whole weekend to get used to the idea.

On Saturday night, Gramps and I took the bus and the monorail to Seattle Center. Gramps looked better than he had the last time we went to Seattle Center. It wasn't just because he was wearing his teeth, either. I wasn't quite sure what it was.

"You look real nice, Gramps."

"Thanks. I thought I should look presentable to help you find the boy with the skateboard. Your mother ironed this white shirt for me."

"It's a nice shirt." My brain was getting confused. What if the boy with the skateboard really was there? I know I told Gramps that's why I wanted him to take me back, but it was just to get Gramps to dance with those ladies.

Or was it?

Six

🐂

"Where do you want to sit, Gramps?" We stood next to the band and looked at the tables surrounding the dance floor. Jerry Sweeney and the Sweetnotes were playing something I had never heard before. Gramps seemed to know it though; he was smiling and tapping his foot. Then, in the middle of the song, all of a sudden, all the Sweetnotes put their horns down and shouted, "PENN-SYLVANIA SIX FIVE OH OH OH!" A lot of the people shouted it with the band — even Gramps! Then the band played more of the song. I guess the shouting was part of it. Pretty strange.

"Gramps? Don't you want to sit down?" I was not crazy about spending the evening standing next to the Sweetnotes with their horns blaring in my ear.

Gramps pointed to an empty table across the dance floor. "How 'bout right over there?"

"Okay." I started walking toward it, but Gramps put his hand on my shoulder.

"Janie, just wait until the song's over, then we can walk across the dance floor. It's more polite."

"Okay." I was glad Gramps seemed to know how to act at this kind of dance, because I sure didn't. While we waited, I checked it out; just like last time, there were more ladies than men. They had on pretty dresses, and a lot of them were sitting at tables, tapping their toes. If I could just figure out a way to get Gramps to ask one of them to dance — I was sure they'd cooperate. Those ladies seemed dying to get out there.

We found a table, but Gramps seemed nervous about sitting down. He asked me if I wanted anything to eat. I guess he needed a project.

"I'd like an Orange Julius, if that's okay."

"Coming up. I'll be right back."

The Sweetnotes took a break, and people started milling around. I saw one lady wearing a little red hat bouncing off the dance floor. I bet she was almost a hundred! Pretty amazing. This seemed to be a cool place for senior citizens, but it wasn't for me. I felt dumb sitting there. I didn't see another kid in the whole place.

As Gramps sat down with the Orange Juliuses, he whispered, "I found the boy with the skateboard."

"You did?" I tried to act interested. Actually, it wasn't too hard.

"Yep. He was in front of me in line. Then he went to that table at the end of the room —" Gramps pointed.

"Gramps!" I pushed his hand down.

"Oops, sorry, Janie." Gramps patted my hand. "Well, now that we've spotted him, we'll have to figure out how to get you two together."

"I've got a better idea."

"What's that?"

"While we're trying to figure out how I'm supposed to meet the boy with the skateboard, why don't you ask a lady to dance?"

Gramps frowned and looked down at the floor.

"Gramps, you're the one who said friends don't come down the chimney."

"That's different."

"What's different about it?"

"The lady might say no —"

"So what? Then you just ask another one. I think you should ask every third lady to dance." As soon as I said that, the music started up again. "See, Gramps —" I started to point at a lady.

"Janie!" Gramps covered my hand with his.

"Sorry. But see that lady? She's tapping her foot. You just know she's dying to dance."

"I'll make a deal with you." Gramps swallowed and looked toward the end of the room. "The boy with the skateboard is sitting next to the same lady he was with last time. If you walk over there with me to talk to him, I'll ask her to dance."

I was trapped; if I said no, I was sure that I'd never get Gramps to dance with anyone. I looked up at him in his nice white shirt and thought about how he was wearing his teeth and everything, and I knew I had to go with him. "Well, okay — I guess so."

Gramps waited for the music to stop, and then he got up and I followed him across the floor to where they were sitting. My heart started thumping like the drum in the band. "Gramps," I whispered, "I'm scared."

"Me, too," he whispered back.

"What if they don't want to talk to us?"

"We'll leave and get another Orange Julius."

"Okay," I whispered.

I stood next to Gramps when he got to their table, and I tried not to look ridiculous, as if going up to strange guys was something I did all the time.

"Uh — well, uh — are you enjoying yourselves?" Gramps asked the lady.

"Oh my, yes," she smiled at Gramps and her eyes sparkled. "I wouldn't miss one of these for the world. I just love the music, although my grandson brings his own." She motioned to the boy with the skateboard, who was sitting next to her with his earphones on. I looked around, wondering what to do. I felt like an idiot.

Gramps cleared his throat. "Well, uh — would you care to dance?"

"I'm sorry — I don't hear too well." She motioned to the hearing aid she was wearing. I could hardly hear Gramps myself, he'd been mumbling so quietly.

I gave him a little poke. "Louder, Gramps."

"Dance? Would you like to have the next dance?" This time he spoke up a lot better.

"I'd love that, Mr. —"

"Bliss, George P. Bliss. This is my granddaughter, Jane Higgins."

"Hi," I mumbled.

"I'm Pearl Birdwell, and this —" she poked the boy with the skateboard —"take that off, Brady — this is my grandson Brady Birdwell."

He took the earphones off, and the band music started up. His grandmother motioned to me as she got up to dance with Gramps. "Keep my seat warm for me, dear."

I slid into her seat and watched while Gramps and Mrs. Birdwell walked out on the dance floor. He held out his arms to her, and soon they were dancing around just like everyone else. It made me so happy to watch them. Mrs. Birdwell was chatting away and Gramps was smiling. Brady and I just sat there staring at the dance floor. I wished I could think of something to say to him.

"How are you?" I finally blurted out.

"Fine." He picked up his skateboard and twirled the wheels around. "Uh — how are you?"

"Fine." Then we sat there some more. I couldn't think of any more conversation. I felt totally dumb.

Brady kept twirling his skateboard wheels. Then he said, "Music's lousy, isn't it?"

"Yeah, it's pretty strange." I looked over at him. He probably wanted to put his Walkman back on so he didn't have to talk to me. "Uh — I can see why you bring your own."

"It's the only way I can stand these things."

"Yeah." I started wondering why he came here. After what seemed like an hour, I got up my nerve to ask. "Uh — why do you come, then?"

"I bring my grandmother. She's crazy about these dances. My parents don't want her riding the bus down here alone." He smiled. "She always jokes that I'm supposed to chaperone her and protect her from pushy gentlemen."

That made me laugh. "Well, she doesn't have to worry about Gramps. He's pretty shy."

Brady handed me the earphones. "Wanna listen?"

"Sure, thanks." Instead of staring at the dance floor, I looked at him when he handed me his Walkman. He had freckles and brown eyes. Sort of cute. I couldn't believe I was actually talking to him. "What station do you like?" I asked.

"KZOK."

"Me, too." I smiled as I put the earphones over my head. It was weird, watching the old people dance to the reggae song I was hearing. After that a rap song came on, and they really looked funny dancing to that. When it was over, I gave his Walkman back to him.

"The band's playing a new song. Looks like they're dancing another one." Brady pointed at his grandmother and Gramps. Then he looked at his watch. "We're going to have to leave pretty soon so we can get the bus."

"Where do you live?"

"Ballard, near the locks." Brady reached down and picked up his skateboard. "I'd like to figure out a way to get Hershel out of there."

"He's that sea lion that swims around the locks and eats all the salmon, right?" I was pretty sure that's what he meant.

"Yeah. Some people want to blast that blubber out of the water. BANG!" Brady pretended to be shooting.

"I don't think they should shoot him."

"I don't, either. But it was awesome when they threw that dynamite in the water." Brady threw his arms up like a big explosion. "KA-POW!" Then he wound the cord around his Walkman. "What school do you go to?"

"Martin Luther King. I'm in seventh."

"Me too — at Lakeview."

Gramps and Mrs. Birdwell came off the dance floor. For once Gramps didn't look all gray. His cheeks were even kind of rosy. I hoped the exercise wasn't too much for him.

Mrs. Birdwell looked at her watch. "Well, Brady — we don't want to turn into pumpkins." She winked at me. "My carriage awaits at Fifth and Denny."

"We need to be on our way, too." Gramps put his hand on my shoulder. "Got to tear ourselves away, Janie."

The four of us rode down the escalator and waved good-bye as Brady and Mrs. Birdwell turned north toward Fifth Avenue, and Gramps and I headed for the monorail.

All the way to the monorail, Gramps was whistling the Pennsylvania six five oh oh oh song, and I was humming the reggae music.

Going home on the bus, Gramps told me that Pearl lived with her son Mike, who was Brady's father, and Marla, Brady's mother. Mike was the manager at Kmart and Marla worked as a secretary in a doctor's office. Brady also had an older brother, Alex, who was fourteen. Pearl's husband had died four years ago, Gramps also found out.

I thought he sure got a lot of information in just a couple of dances. All I found out was that Brady didn't want Hershel the sea lion to get shot and that he liked KZOK. Also that he was in the seventh grade at Lakeview. I guess that was a start. Actually, the more I thought about it, the more I realized it was pretty amazing. It was the first real conversation I'd had with a boy without Alicia. I couldn't quite believe it. I thought about Brady Birdwell all the way home.

Only the porch light was on when we got home. John was spending the night at Kevin Wong's house, and Mom and Dad had gone out to a movie. Gramps and I made ourselves a peanut butter sandwich to split before we went to bed.

Gramps took a bite out of the sandwich. "I think it would be a good idea to go back to the next dance."

I gave Juliet a little piece of my sandwich. "Me, too." I smiled at Gramps and he grinned. His teeth sure looked terrific.

If someone had told me that when I was twelve I'd be excited about going to senior citizens dances, I would have thought they were crazy.

Seven

The time has come, I decided Monday morning as I marched along to the bus stop. I would put the Jane G. Higgins Popularity Plan into action. To convince myself to do it, I kept going over my conversation with Brady Birdwell. We hadn't said much, but every word of it made me happy. I told myself I hadn't known him before, and we ended up actually having a real conversation, so it couldn't be too hard to just say hi to people I didn't know at school. I made up my own little slogan: Just say hi.

All the way to the bus stop, over and over, I kept reminding myself, "Just say hi," hoping that by the time I got to school, I'd be able to go for it.

As I was waiting for the bus, Rhonda and Nalita came up. They were laughing and whispering. Would they notice me? I tried not to act as if I cared or anything, because one thing people can't stand is a creep who's too eager or butts in. I put a look on my face that I hoped wasn't unfriendly but would seem like I was one of the cool people, too. But it didn't matter; I might as well have been part of the bushes. Brian and Darrell came charging up just as the bus came, and they all crowded on together ahead of me, even though I had been there first. I climbed up the steps and sat alone behind the bus driver. I was sure only nerds sat behind the bus driver, but I couldn't stand the idea of walking down the aisle to find a seat with everyone looking at me.

Maybe my plan was the dumbest idea I'd ever had. Just say hi — how pitiful. I tried to think about Brady Birdwell again to get my confidence back, but what if the only reason he talked to me was because I was the only other person in the place under seventy?

When the bus pulled up in front of school, I wanted to stay on it and just go home. I sat there and waited while almost everyone got off. Then the bus driver turned around and stared at me, so I left, too. As I went down the front steps, I noticed a girl getting off at the back. She was shorter than I was and quite pudgy and all by herself. Probably a nerd, like me.

"Hi," I blurted out and then raced into the school without looking back. She probably thought I was crazy.

On my way to homeroom, I had this whole conversation in my head. "Quit the plan, it's dumb."

"But I haven't even tried it."

"It won't work."

"How can I be sure unless I do it?"

"Without Alicia you are no one."

"But Brady Birdwell talked to me."

That thought made me feel a little better. I finally decided I couldn't quit the plan until I gave it an official try, but it would be a pretend try — I was too scared to really do it.

I walked down the hall, looked at every third person, and imagined I was saying "Hi." The first one was a huge guy in a Seahawks shirt who looked like a ninth-grader, then three people after that was a tall, skinny girl with stringy hair and purple lipstick, walking along looking at the floor, then three people after that was this shrimpy red-haired guy, jumping around, punching his friend in the arm.

By the time I got to homeroom, I was totally bummed out. There was no way I could have said hi to any of them. The ninth-grade guy was too big, the girl was staring at the floor, and the shrimpy guy was bouncing around too much. I knew that if there was any hope at all, I'd have to revise the plan if I was going to get it off the ground. Even at that, I wasn't sure I'd ever do it. I made some doodles in my notebook, then I wrote down on the corner of the paper:

> 1. Say hi to every third person who:
>   a. is not too tall
>   b. seems like a seventh-grader
>   c. is a girl

While Mr. Chung was reading the bulletin, my mind started wandering once more to Brady Birdwell, and I remembered everything about the dance all over again. It had been scary walking up to him and Mrs. Birdwell. Gramps was brave to ask her to dance, even if he did mumble. "Jane," I said to myself, "when you made yourselves go up to them, you ended up having a great time. Now that the plan is just seventh-grade girls, it'll be easier. Just do it!"

The bell rang. I gathered up my books and hung around, pretending to read the blackboard, until everyone left. It seemed easier to start my plan without everyone in my homeroom watching. I peeked around the door and took a deep breath. I had waited so long that the hall was almost empty. I turned left and started walking to my math class.

One. The first person I passed was a pretty black girl with dreadlocks and a cool leather jacket. Definitely not a seventh-grader. No problem — I didn't have to say a thing. I kept going, my eyes scanning the halls. Number two was a guy carrying a clarinet case. Three was another guy. Saved. Then I spotted this girl walking with another girl; no lipstick, about my height, probably seventh grade. She was wearing a jeans jacket and a button with some rock guy's picture on it, although I couldn't see who it was from there. This was it.

"Hi," I squeaked, and scurried along next to the lockers. Out of the corner of my eye, I saw her friend ask "Who's that?" and she just shrugged. I got to my math class just as the bell rang. I slipped into my seat. Then I realized she hadn't been the third person. She was the fourth — I'd already screwed up the plan. Oh, well, I thought. At least I had actually done it!

Between math and language arts I hung back again until the halls were almost empty. I passed two girls who looked like seventh-graders, but I didn't have to say hi to them because it was every third person. I thought I had escaped having to do it, but just as I got to language arts, a girl went by; Asian, wearing bright pink earrings, a pink-and-black sweatshirt, shorter than me — not sure what grade. "Just do it!" I told myself.

"Hi," I gasped and bolted into class.

During language arts I decided this would win a prize for the most nerve-racking morning of my life. Lunch period was next. I'd never be able to eat and keep up my plan, so I bagged it until the afternoon.

I don't know what I hated more about seventh grade — lunch period, when I ate alone, or the ride to school, when my seat behind the bus driver seemed like a desert island. It was a toss-up. At least in class, especially where we had assigned seats, it wasn't so noticeable that I didn't have any friends.

I looked around for a seat at lunch. There were some empty chairs at the end of a table of enormous ninth-grade guys. They were very loud, yelling at each other with deep voices. They pounded each other and horsed around. Some had hairy faces. They were all bunched at one end of the table, and I slipped into a chair near the wall. No one could see me with their big bodies blocking me from the whole rest of the lunchroom. But in case anyone noticed me, I wanted to look like I was studying for a test, so I opened my notebook while I ate my tuna sandwich.

I reviewed my plan and decided that it would make it more interesting if I put down what the responses were. How wonderful it would be if I got some hi's back! I made two columns on the paper and put the date at the top. I headed one column with "F.P." for Friendly Person (if the person said hi back to me) and the other with "ZILCH" (if there was no response). Two checks for the ZILCH column.

I wadded up my lunch bag, tossed it in the garbage, and went back to my seat to wait for the bell. I sat there for a while after it rang, just as I had done in the morning. The uncrowded halls definitely made the plan a lot easier.

Between lunch and P.E. the only candidate was a black girl with glasses. After I said "Hi," she looked at me like I was a fool, which was what I felt like. On the way to science I didn't wait long enough, and the halls were more crowded. I made myself say "Hi" to a blonde girl with her hair in a French braid and then three people later another blonde girl with a lot of pimples. They both acted like they hadn't heard me.

"Whoops!" As I turned the corner I practically bumped into another seventh-grade–looking girl; very skinny, frizzy black hair, braces — the third person. "Uh — hi." Even though I stammered, my voice didn't squeak as much this time. Maybe I was getting used to it.

"Hi." She smiled and then looked away real quick.

In science I whipped out my notebook and made a nice big check in the F.P. column. My first one. I looked at it for a moment, then closed my notebook. Ta-da! Progress!

When I left science for woodshop, a girl approached me from her class across the hall. It was the very first girl I had said hi to that morning, the one with the jeans jacket with the rock button. She was actually coming toward me! The plan was working!

"Hey, how do you know me?" she yelled across the hall.

I froze and stared at her. Then, thank goodness, I remembered what the plan called for in this situation. "Uh — I — well, didn't you go to Hidden Valley Camp?" I said, as casually as I could.

"Not me."

"You look like Juliet — somebody I know from there." I mumbled. Our dog's name was the only one I could think of.

"Yeah, well — see ya."

Whew. As I went into class, I told myself that if this happened again, I'd say it a lot smoother. The first time had to be the hardest.

I had no idea that I'd have another chance to practice that part so soon, but on the way to the bus stop, the

Asian girl with the pink earrings and the pink-and-black sweatshirt passed me. "Did you go to Rockmount?"

"No. Evergreen."

"Then where'd you know me from? You don't go to Blaine Methodist — do you?"

"No. Didn't you go to Hidden Valley Camp?"

"No. Just church camp."

"Oh, well, you look like Juliet — someone I knew from Hidden Valley." I had been right, it was a lot easier this time. She left and I climbed on the bus. I didn't mind sitting by myself as much because I opened my notebook and looked at my progress sheet. Five zilches and one F.P. It hadn't been a total disaster! Plus, those two girls had asked me how I knew them, and we had some little conversations, even if my part had been lies. I had made a start!

Gramps was watching TV when I got home. I stuck my head in his door.

"Hi!"

"Hi, Janie. How was school?"

"I took your advice." I smiled. "I said hi to some people."

"Good for you." Gramps stood up and patted me on the back.

John tore out of his room wearing his soccer shoes. He was probably late for practice, as usual. "Hi, Janie."

It was nice to have people say hi to me and say my name, even if they were in my own family. I didn't even mention to John that he wasn't supposed to wear his soccer shoes in the house.

"Good luck at practice."

"Thanks." He grinned and pointed at his shoes. "Don't tell Mom."

"Okay." I went into Gramps's room and sat next to him in front of the TV. Gramps watches the news a lot on CNN. A commercial came on, but instead of turning the sound off like he always does, Gramps turned it up.

"SEND IN NOW FOR THIS FAMOUS COLLECTION OF TWENTY-FIVE BEST-LOVED WALTZES." While the announcer talked, it showed a couple dancing around to corny music. "ONLY NINETEEN NINETY-FIVE — JUST CALL THIS TOLL-FREE NUMBER AND THE COLLECTION CAN BE YOURS. THIS WONDERFUL COLLECTION IS NOT AVAILABLE ANYWHERE ELSE. HURRY WHILE THEY LAST. 1-800-555-6393. CALL TODAY FOR THE DANCE MUSIC EVERYONE LOVES."

"You know, I sure like those songs —" Gramps slipped a little notebook from his pocket and jotted down the number.

"Are you going to call up and get them?"

"Just might do that." Gramps stuck the notebook back in his pocket. "Guess I'll have to think about it a bit. I got a credit card when I opened my bank account here. I've never used it but — I suppose it's still good."

Gramps switched the TV to "Jeopardy!" and we watched that for a while. Then he flipped back over to CNN. Another commercial was on.

"GLAMOUR-LENGTH PRESS-ON NAILS FOR THE GLAMOUR LOOK YOU'VE ALWAYS DREAMED OF. THE SOPHISTICATION OF MODELS AND HOLLYWOOD STARS IS YOURS IN SECONDS FOR ONLY NINE NINETY-FIVE. MONEY-BACK GUARANTEE IF NOT COMPLETELY SATISFIED. CALL THIS TOLL-FREE NUMBER FOR INSTANT GLAMOUR. 1-800-555-6393."

I noticed that it was the same number that Gramps wrote down for the twenty-five best-loved waltzes. I looked down at my nails. They were pretty scuzzy. I had always wanted beautiful long fingernails — but mine never got that way. I bit them sometimes without even knowing it. I began imagining myself polishing those glamour-length nails with a gorgeous color — I bet I'd look like some of those ninth grade girls I saw in the bathroom.

"Gramps —"

"What is it, Janie?"

"If you call up that number, I think I'd like to get some of those fingernails."

Gramps didn't say anything for a minute.

"I think I have about ten dollars in my bank from baby-sitting and watering our neighbor's plants. I'll have to check for sure."

Gramps reached in his wallet and took out his credit card. "We'll do it. I'll call 'em right now. But I want to pay for both the waltzes and the fingernails. I might as well spend my money — as they say, you can't take it with you." He chuckled as he went down the hall to Mom and Dad's room to use the phone.

While Gramps was ordering the stuff, I imagined being at the next dance and having those long gorgeous fingernails, holding my Orange Julius, tapping on the table, and — holding Brady Birdwell's hand. Wow . . . wouldn't I really have something to write Alicia!

Eight

The next few days at school, the plan was zinging right along. There were still more checks in the ZILCH column than in the F.P. column, but every time I got a "Hi" back, I got more confidence. By Thursday I had twelve zilches but I had four F.P.'s. Not bad!

I was on my way to my locker before lunch, when I passed two girls I had talked to the first day of the plan. The blonde girl in the jeans jacket with the rock button was talking to the Asian girl who had worn the pink earrings and the pink-and-black sweatshirt. The Asian girl pointed at me.

"Hi!" I said, cheerily, hoping I sounded like a popular person, as I walked by. I couldn't tell if they said anything back to me, because just then a whole bunch of people streamed out from the room next to my locker.

When the crowd cleared out, I overheard the two of them talking. My locker door blocked me from them so they didn't know I was still there.

"Do you know that girl who just went by —"

"No."

"I don't, either — the other day she told me I looked like someone named Juliet who went to camp with her."

"You must be kidding!"

"Why?"

"She said the exact same thing to me!"

"Some Juliet person, too? That is so weird."

"We don't look anything alike —"

"That's for sure!"

"What a nerd. That girl is strange!" They both cracked up, laughing their heads off.

I stuck my head in my locker as far as I could, waiting for them to leave. The metal at the back of my locker was cold against my forehead. "Please, don't let them see me," I said, silently. I had trouble breathing; it was dark and stuffy in there, and tears stung my eyes. *They were right. I was a nerd.* It felt suffocating in my locker, but I wished I could get my entire body inside. I could hear people going by, laughing and talking, so I waited with my head jammed against the back until it got quiet. Finally when I thought the hall was empty, I pulled my head out.

I yanked open my notebook and grabbed the page with the ZILCH column and the F.P. column and ripped it out. I smashed it into a little ball and threw it in the bottom of my locker and slammed the door.

I slunk into the lunchroom and sat at the same table where I had been sitting all week, hiding in the corner behind the ninth-grade boys. I took my sandwich, my apple, the juice, and the cookie out of the bag and stared at it. Then I just opened the bag and put it all back, except for the cookie.

All I could think about were the good old days at Evergreen when I used to have Alicia to hang around with; those times after school, when we'd meet at our tree, polishing off a whole bag of Doritos and whispering about the stuff we'd never tell anyone else. Like what guys we thought were cute and whether you should get a bra if you didn't really need one; stuff like that. I sat there, slowly chewing my cookie, remembering those times. I never knew how much you could miss a person. And I never knew a place could be as miserable as King Junior High.

To keep from crying and to remind myself that I did have a friend in this world, I took a piece of paper out of my notebook and started a letter to Alicia — even though I still hadn't gotten another one from her.

Dear Alicia,
How is California? I figured you must be having
a great time since I haven't heard from you. I've
been having a great time, too. I went to a dance!
It was at Seattle Center and I met this neat guy,
Brady Birdwell, who goes to Lakeview Junior
High. We danced every dance — it was so great!
School is great too, I'm meeting a lot of new
people from all the other elementary schools.
Everything is so fun here! Well, don't do anything
I wouldn't do — HA! HA!

The lies just seemed to roll off my pen like the last time, but I didn't even care. Who'd want to read the truth? Just as I was about to sign my name to the letter, I thought I heard someone say "Hi." I knew they couldn't be talking to me, so I kept looking at my letter. Then I heard it again. I looked up.

"Hi. Uh — would it be okay if I sat with you?"

I looked around. There was no one at the end of the

table — she had to mean me! "Yes!" I said, almost shouting.

It was the short, pudgy girl from the bus; the very first one I had said hi to. I had never been so happy to see anyone in my whole life. She sat across from me and opened her lunch bag. I began to feel a little hungrier, so I pulled my sandwich out of my bag, too. I tried to think of something to say. Alicia would have plunged right in, talking like mad, but I just sat there, munching my sandwich, wishing I could think of some way to start a conversation. Finally, I thought of something.

"You didn't go to Evergreen, did you?" I asked.

"No. We just moved here from Idaho Falls."

"That's in Idaho?" Then I felt embarrassed. "Pretty stupid — where else would it be." I laughed.

She laughed, too. "What street do you live on? I live on Hunter Boulevard."

"Just a few blocks from there, on Court. I'm Janie Higgins. Who're you?"

"Carly Reese — I really hated having to move."

"Moving stinks," I said emphatically.

We sat there, eating our sandwiches, and talked a little bit more. Carly talked about what it had been like in Idaho Falls, and I talked about Evergreen. It wasn't as easy as talking to Alicia; maybe nothing would ever be as easy as that. But it wasn't as hard as I thought, once I got started. The bell rang as I was finishing my sandwich. "Well, guess we better get to class."

"On to P.E. for me." Carly crumpled up her lunch bag and hesitated for a minute. "Thanks for letting me sit with you."

I grinned. "Want to sit together tomorrow?"

"Great!"

We walked through the lunchroom together. At the

75

door we waved and went in opposite directions. "See you later," I called over my shoulder.

That afternoon things got better and better. The girl with the braces and the dark brown frizzy hair said hi to me first when I was on my way to P.E. Then another one of my F.P.'s from Tuesday, a thin black girl with corn braids, also said hi first. In my last-period class I thought about what a roller-coaster day it had been. When those girls called me a nerd, I thought I was doomed; my life as a seventh-grader was all downhill. Now things were really looking up — there was hope!

After school I had to rush to the bus because Mr. Letterby made the whole science class stay five minutes after the bell. I was almost the last one to climb on. I started to slip into the empty seat behind the driver as usual, when Carly waved from the seat on the left side. "Janie! Sit over here," she called, picking up her books off the seat next to her.

I practically skipped down the aisle. "Thanks!" I scooted in next to her. I couldn't believe I had someone to sit with; not only that — she'd saved me a seat!

"Letterby — my science teacher — made us stay after the bell. I was afraid I'd miss the bus," I told her.

"I have him for science second period. He did that to us, too — what a bummer." Carly sat up in the seat and cleared her throat. "There's been entirely too much talking. Since I don't know who the culprits are — the whole class will suffer!" she said, in a snarly voice that sounded just like Letterby. I cracked up.

We found out we had the same teachers for a few of our other classes, too. Carly also did an imitation of Miss Burke, the P.E. teacher, that was hilarious. Best of all, we gave each other our phone numbers before she had to get off at her stop. I stared at the scrap of notebook paper with her number on it all the way home.

When I got home, Gramps met me at the door. He was holding a brown box. "Janie, when I ordered our merchandise from the television, I paid extra so they'd send it two-day air."

"You did?" I was surprised that Gramps had been in so much of a hurry. "That's it?"

"Yep. Must be — it says Special Promotions, and it has a return address from New Jersey. Let's open it."

"All right!" I followed him into the kitchen. Gramps put the box on the kitchen table and got a knife to cut the sides with. Inside the box were zillions of Styrofoam peanuts. We started laughing as we dug through the peanuts. Gramps pulled out the Twenty-five Best-Loved Waltzes, and right underneath was the box of fingernails. Glamour-length press-on nails, just like we had ordered.

"Wow. I can wear these to the next dance —"

"Let's go Saturday."

"Good idea." I hugged Gramps. Then I ran up to my room. I couldn't wait to go to Pay 'n Save and get some beautiful nail polish. I thought about Carly — it would be great if she wanted to go with me and help pick it out. But then I wondered if someone from Idaho Falls would think experimenting with nail polish and makeup was dumb. Maybe when she found out that was one of my ideas of a good time, she'd decide we had nothing in common.

I took the nails out of the box; they were oval-shaped plastic things. I thought nine ninety-five seemed a lot of money for ten little pieces of plastic. I'd have to be careful not to lose them — at that price, each fingernail cost almost a dollar! I was fiddling around with them when Gramps stuck his head in my room.

"Janie." He smiled, his eyes twinkling. "Would you like to listen to the waltzes?"

"Love to." I hopped up and followed him to the living room. It was wonderful seeing Gramps excited. I sat on the couch and watched him carefully slip the record from the jacket and put it on the stereo. "This is a fine one," he said, as the first song started. Then Gramps sang with the record, "*I-was-dan-cing-with-my-dar-ling-to-the-Ten-nes-see-Waltz* —" He walked to the couch and held out his hand. "May I have this dance, ma'am?"

"I don't know how, Gramps."

"Well, we'll fix that. Come on — I'll show you."

"Uh — I, well —" I looked down at the floor. "I feel stupid."

Gramps looked around the living room. "No one here but us chickens. We all have to start somewhere." Gramps hummed along with the song and held his other hand out.

"Well, I hope I don't step on your feet." I took his hands and he pulled me up and led me to the middle of the living room.

"The lady puts her left arm on the gentleman's shoulder," he explained.

"I can't reach your shoulder, Gramps," I said, stretching my arm up.

"On my arm will do. Then the gentleman puts his right arm around her waist, and he holds her left hand with his right. Ready?"

I nodded.

"Now. It's one-two-three, one-two-three. You step around like a little box." Gramps showed me the steps and I copied him, watching our feet.

"Dan-cing-with-my-dar-ling" — Gramps sang — *"when-an-old* — oops!" I had stepped on his toe. "Never mind, you're doing great. *An-old-friend-I-hap-pened-to-meet —"* Gramps sang louder.

I had to keep watching our feet, but pretty soon I began to get it. I could look up once in a while and still do the steps. *"When-an-old-friend-I-hap-pened-to-meet,"* I even sang with Gramps. We glided round and round . . . and pretty soon I didn't have to look at my feet — it was great! Then I heard someone laughing.

"It's the Lawrence Welk show!" John poked his head around the living room door and completely cracked up.

Gramps and I didn't care. We just laughed, too, and kept dancing, and as we sailed all over the living room, I wondered what it would really be like to dance — to slow-dance . . . with Brady Birdwell.

Nine

At the bus stop the next day, I didn't even mind when Nalita and Rhonda acted like I was part of the bushes. I was looking forward to seeing Carly. For a minute I worried that maybe she had found some cool people to be with and would dump me; but when I got on the bus she was sitting alone and waved the minute she saw me. I was so relieved! I followed Nalita and Rhonda down the aisle. They ignored Carly as they walked to the back. They probably thought anyone who wanted to be with me wasn't cool. But then I wondered, would Carly want to be with me outside of school? Sometimes that's a whole different deal; people can be friendly at school, but after the last bell rings each day, you're history. Maybe she had given me her phone number just to be polite.

"Thanks for saving me a seat." I smiled as I sat next to her.

"I couldn't wait till we got to your stop. I hate sitting alone." She glanced toward the back of the bus, where the popular people sat. It sounded like party time back there.

Carly seemed so happy to see me that I thought I'd take a chance about the nail polish. But then I lost my nerve. Just do it, I told myself. Finally I blurted out, "I was wondering if you'd like to go to Pay 'n Save with me sometime before Saturday?"

"Sure — the one on Rainier?"

"That's the one — we could walk there. I want to buy some nail polish, and I need someone to help me pick out a good color." I noticed Carly glancing at my hands. She probably wondered what there was to polish; each of my raggedy fingernails looked like they'd take only a puny drip. "I bought some press-on nails," I explained.

"I always wanted those — after you bite your nails, you'd just stick on those nice nails, and who'd ever know that underneath you'd practically destroyed your hand."

"My idea — exactly!" I looked down at my nails. I couldn't wait for each stubby mess to get covered up. "I just wish I knew what color to get. You could go broke getting some color that looks gorgeous on the chart —"

"And looks disgusting when you get it on at home." Carly laughed. "I've blown more money on ugly lipstick that way. But if you want to mess around with nail polish, my mom has a lot. Why don't you come over to my house and we could fool around with hers? Then you might know what you'd like."

The bus pulled up in front of school, and we stood up to get out. "That would be neat. My mom doesn't wear makeup. She only has a couple of crummy lipsticks in the back of her drawer from a hundred years ago that smell funny." We agreed that we'd meet for lunch and go to her house after school.

What a difference! Having Carly to be with changed my whole feeling about school. But when I got to homeroom, I worried that I could be making the same mistake that I had made with Alicia — just hanging around one person. If Carly moved again, or got sick and missed school — I'd be right back where I started: doomed to misery. But I knew I wasn't going to continue the Jane G. Higgins Popularity Plan of saying hi to every third girl who looked like a seventh-grader. Having a plan to get popular seemed so dumb now. I'd be happy to have just a few real friends. So to meet more people, I decided that whenever I felt like it, I'd say hi to people who looked like they didn't have anybody to be with. Who knows? Maybe there'd be someone who'd like a friendly hello.

At lunch, I was walking into the lunchroom when the girl with the frizzy brown hair and braces came through the door next to me. She looked around. I wasn't sure, but I didn't think she was meeting anyone.

"I sit over in the corner — if you want to sit there, too." I smiled. I hadn't planned on asking people to sit with Carly and me, but why not mention it? After all, she had been my first F.P. when I had been doing the plan, and she did look all alone.

"Thanks — what's your name again?" She flashed a huge silver grin.

I told her my name and found out she was Jessica Valdez. Carly got to the table a few minutes after we did, and it turned out that she and Jessica had the same language arts class. They joked around about their teacher, Mr. Klecko, whose pants had a little rip in the seat that he didn't even know about. Every time he turned to write on the board, the whole class pointed to it. Carly and Jessica said it was hilarious.

When we got to Carly's house after school, we went into her mom's room, and she pulled five different colors of nail polish out of the drawer.

"Are you sure it's okay just to take your mom's stuff like this?" I asked.

"No problem. Mom always lets me borrow her makeup. I wish I could wear some of her clothes, but I'm too fat."

It's funny about people. When I first saw Carly, I had thought about her as the pudgy girl on the bus. I'm sure the popular kids saw her that way, too; but now I was hardly even aware of her being overweight. It seems like when you get to know someone, you just don't think about those things. "I think your clothes look real good on you."

Carly smiled. "Want to try on some of her lipsticks?"

"Great —" I stared into the drawer. It looked like the makeup department at Nordstrom's. "This is really something. She sure has a lot to pick from."

"She still wears the ones in the front, but we can use any of these." Carly pointed to a bunch in the back of the drawer and scooped up a handful of lipstick. I carried the nail polish and polish remover into her room. What a fantastic afternoon! Dab on Pink Delight, wipe it off . . . dab, dab . . . Hot Coral . . . wipe, wipe, dab, dab . . . Firelight Orange . . . wipe, wipe, dab, dab . . . That Old Red Magic . . . wipe, wipe, dab, dab . . . Cherries in the Snow — my favorite. It even had matching nail polish. I hated when it was time to leave and I had to take it off. I sighed, wiped my mouth, and began working on my nails with the polish remover.

"Yuk. This stuff stinks. I wish I could just leave my nails polished, this color is so pretty."

"Just take the bottle with you — take this, too." She handed me the Cherries in the Snow lipstick.

"Thanks a bunch! Are you sure your mom won't mind?"

"Nope. Mom never wears dark red anymore."

"My mom's against makeup." I explained all about Mom's speeches. "I have to try it on when she's at work."

"So that's why you act like I just gave you a handful of diamonds." Carly laughed.

When I got home, John and Kevin were in John's room. They were talking loudly and seemed very excited.

"Take the filter out — then try it."

"Will that reverse it?"

"It's awesome! Just wait!"

I heard this funny noise — some kind of machine. Then they shrieked and yelled, "It's working! It's shooting! It's shooting!" Then John's door slammed. Thank goodness I had spent the afternoon at Carly's, instead of having to listen to those two.

In my room, I flopped down on my bed and gazed at the bottle of nail polish. What a beautiful color. I decided to cut little fingernail-shaped pieces out of index cards and tape them on and then polish them to try the whole thing out before I polished the press-on nails. Before I did that, I experimented with another hair style, using a lot of gel, and put on the lipstick Carly had given me. Then I made the practice nails and polished them. As I was finishing doing the little finger of the last hand, I heard the phone ring. John didn't answer it, so I went to get it. As I left my room, I glanced in the mirror. I had never realized how sophisticated makeup could make a person look.

As I walked down the hall to Mom's room, John's door flew open.

WHOOOWHOOOOMMMMM. I heard this roaring noise and I jumped back against the wall.

"Vaporize the alien!"

"YIIIIIIIIKES!" Styrofoam peanuts sprayed out like a blizzard from the hose of Dad's shop vacuum cleaner.

John and Kevin pointed the hose at me. "Vaporize the alien! Vaporize the — ha ha ha!" Then they fell over laughing, and the hose shot at the ceiling. The peanuts whooooshed up, banged the ceiling, and then bounced down all over the place.

"YOU LITTLE CREEPS!"

John and Kevin rolled around holding their sides.

"I'LL VAPORIZE YOU — YOU SCUM!" I grabbed the hose and blasted both of them with those little peanuts. When the last piece of Styrofoam shot out of the vacuum cleaner, I dumped the hose on their heads and stomped down the hall to my room.

When I looked in the mirror, I almost died. The Cherries in the Snow looked like snow balls and rotten fruit. The nail polish was smeared in blobby streaks, and those horrible little white things were stuck everywhere. My hair looked like I had giant dandruff. John Higgins would pay for this. I didn't know what I would do, but I'd get revenge somehow.

I heard the garage open just a minute later, and I tore down the stairs to the back door.

"Mom! John and Kevin shot —"

"What in the world happened to you!" Mom put the bag of groceries down on the counter. She looked like she was in shock.

"That's what I'm trying to tell you! John and Kevin shot —"

"You look awful! What is all that red stuff?" Mom stared at me.

"Cherries in the Snow — John and Kevin shot —"

"We don't have any cherries — Janie, what in the world are you talking about?"

"JOHN AND KEVIN SHOT ME WITH DAD'S VACUUM CLEANER!"

"Now, there's no need to yell — they did what?"

"They filled up Dad's shop vacuum cleaner from the garage with those Styrofoam peanuts that came in the box of the stuff Gramps and I sent in for and shot me with it."

"Oh, no! Then what's the red stuff?"

"Nail polish."

"Oh?" Mom raised her eyebrows.

"I borrowed it from my new friend Carly. John better get punished for this!"

"I'll handle it, Janie. Now you better get cleaned up."

I was up in my room getting cleaned up when I heard Mom go into John's room. I opened the door a crack so I could hear. She told Kevin to go home. Then she started talking to John.

"There are two things involved here, John. One, you attacked your sister by spraying her with that Styrofoam. That was a very mean thing to do. Two, you took Dad's vacuum without permission."

Good. Mom was using her nurse voice. And it was her mad nurse voice, which was even better.

"There will be consequences for this behavior. It's simply unacceptable. I have never been one to say, 'Wait until your father gets home' — however, in this case, since you took his vacuum, I will need to discuss it with

86

him, and we will let you know after dinner what the consequences are. Until then you are to stay in your room. Is that clear?"

I didn't hear John answer. He must have nodded or something, because Mom closed his door and I heard her go down to the kitchen. For a minute I was afraid she'd come in my room and make her speech about makeup, now that she knew about the nail polish, but she didn't. Maybe she was too mad at John. I hoped those consequences would make him miserable.

After I got cleaned up, I went into Gramps's room, and we watched TV together. Gramps had on CNN like he usually does. We talked a lot, and I told him about how nice it was to have lunch with Carly and Jessica Valdez. Then a commercial came on. I had noticed that lately Gramps didn't shut the sound off; he listened to commercials.

On TV, a man held up a pot of some kind. "How much would you pay for this Orient Express rice steamer? Don't answer!" The man grabbed some knives. "As a bonus — we're going to add these amazing Ginsu knives. They cut through wood, bricks, wire, and never, that's right, never, need sharpening. Now how much would you pay? Don't answer yet — we're still adding more!" The man held up a little gadget. "This magic vegetable peeler will also be yours; you'll wonder how you ever got along without it AND this beautiful set of steak knives, BUT WAIT, THERE'S MORE, this fantastic orange squeezer." The man punched an orange with a little metal thing and juice dribbled out. "The price? All this is yours for the unbelievable low, low price of twenty-nine ninety-five! That's right, the Orient Express rice steamer, the Ginsu knives, the steak knives, the magic vegetable peeler, and the orange juice squeezer. HURRY NOW, WHILE THE OFFER LASTS! Just call this toll-free number today!"

When the number came on the screen, Gramps took his little book out of his pocket and jotted down the number. Then he went down to Mom's room to use the phone. I guess he'd liked getting the Twenty-five Best-Loved Waltzes so much that he just wanted to order more things.

After Gramps finished phoning, we went downstairs to dinner. Mom told me that John had been grounded for a week. I thought he should be grounded for life.

But since she had at least done something to him for blasting me with those peanuts, I didn't need to think about how to get him back. Anyway, all I could think of was the next dance. I couldn't wait.

Ten

"Gramps?"

"Yes?" Gramps straightened his tie as we walked up to the door of the Center House.

"Are you sure this doesn't look dumb?" I held out my hand and looked down at my press-on nails.

"Very pretty."

"Not too fake?" I stuck out the other hand.

"Couldn't tell it from the real thing." Gramps opened the door for me. We walked over to the escalator and rode up to the dance.

"At home I put my hands in my pockets so Mom wouldn't see." I leaned my hand on the escalator railing and turned back to Gramps, who was riding on the step behind me.

"Well, you know how your mother is. She has her opinions about that sort of thing. Don't exactly know why, don't see the harm, myself." Gramps patted my hand.

The band started just as we got there. Gramps started smiling. "I sure love that 'Little Brown Jug.'"

I knew Gramps wouldn't cross the dance floor until the band was through playing, so I just stood there, sneaking glances at my press-on nails, until it was over. I was also sneaking glances around the room, trying to spot Brady. I thought Gramps was totally into watching the Sweetnotes play, but then I noticed his eyes darting around the tables, too.

"Where do you want to sit?" Gramps asked casually when the song ended, his eyes still scanning the place.

"Oh, I don't care," I mumbled, trying to sound casual, too, but hoping we would go down to the end of the room where Mrs. Birdwell and Brady sat last time. It was early yet; the dance had just started, but I had looked the place over. I didn't see them anywhere.

"How about down there?" Gramps pointed to where they had been last time.

"That might be a good idea," I said, trying to sound cool about it.

Gramps led the way across the dance floor, and we found an empty table. We sat there, and I looked at all the people coming in. I was beginning to get nervous. There was no sign of Brady.

"Gramps?" I whispered.

"Yes?"

"What if they don't come?"

Gramps got a worried look on his face, and he watched the door. "How 'bout an Orange Julius?"

"Okay." I kept my eye on the door while Gramps left to get the drinks. More and more people came in, all with white hair, gray hair, or bald. I had spent hours trying on outfits, fixing my hair, getting the press-on nails right, and I even had on a teeny bit of lipstick. Maybe it had been a big waste of time. Where were they? I was sure Mrs. Pearl Birdwell had said she wouldn't miss one of these for anything.

Gramps came back with our Orange Juliuses. "Any sign of them?" He glanced back and forth, looking over the dance floor and at the door.

I shook my head and twirled the straw around in my Orange Julius.

Suddenly Gramps jumped up. He grinned and waved. Mrs. Birdwell and Brady were waving at us from the top of the escalator! My heart started thumping. Brady carried his skateboard, and his Walkman hung around his neck. I thought he looked completely wonderful. They got off the escalator and walked straight over to us.

"How nice to see you two," Mrs. Birdwell chirped.

"Won't you join us?" Gramps motioned to some chairs next to ours. I smiled at Brady, and we said hi.

"Lovely," Mrs. Birdwell said and sat next to Gramps, and Brady sat next to her.

"Can I get you anything to drink?" Gramps asked Mrs. Birdwell.

"How nice of you. Maybe a little later, George."

George. She was calling him George. I thought that was a good sign. I peeked around Gramps and Mrs. Birdwell at Brady. He had put on his Walkman, his skateboard was upside down on his lap, and he was twirling the wheels around.

Gramps tapped his fingers in time to the music on the arm of the chair. "Would you care to dance, Pearl?"

"I'd be delighted."

Gramps and Mrs. Birdwell stood up. He put out his arm, she took it, and they walked out to the dance floor. I looked across the two empty chairs at Brady. He looked over at me. We both smiled. But we both stayed where we were. I wished he would move over and sit next to me. I was afraid he didn't want to — so I didn't want to just move over next to him. We sat there, staring at the people dancing, for the whole song, with the two empty chairs between us. I looked down at my press-on nails. I felt so dumb.

The song ended and Gramps and Mrs. Birdwell looked over at us. Then she stood on her tiptoes and whispered in Gramps's ear. He sure seemed happy. As I watched them walk back, I was glad we were here for Gramps's sake — even though for me it was turning out to be a big zero.

"Janie —" Gramps took out his wallet. "Pearl and I want to keep dancing." He handed me two dollars. "Could you get me a drink?" Then he gave Brady two dollars. "And you get one for your grandmother. Be sure both of you get something for yourselves while you're at it."

"Okay, thanks." I stood up just as Brady did.

"What do you want, Gran?" he asked Mrs. Birdwell.

"One of those orange juices would be nice."

Brady laughed. "Orange Julius, Gran."

"Yes, orange juices."

Gramps wanted the same thing, so Brady and I headed over to the Orange Julius counter together.

"Gran doesn't hear everything too well."

"You mean 'cause she said orange juices instead of Orange Julius."

"Yeah. She gets stuff like that mixed up a lot."

I noticed that Brady was carrying his skateboard. "How come you took your skateboard?" I asked.

"Someone might steal it. You never know."

"Oh." I didn't say anything, but it was hard to imagine one of the people at the seniors dance ripping off his skateboard. I looked at it while we waited in line. It had stickers all over it that said, Gotcha, Fallout, Visions, Nash, Kryptonic, Schmidt Stick, in all these weird fluorescent colors, and it had special tape stripped across it. He must have spent a lot of time fixing it like that. I guessed it meant a lot to him. "Your skateboard's cool."

"Thanks. It's a Valterra."

"Oh."

"Want to try it?"

"Try it? Uh — now? Tonight?"

"We could go out on the walk in front of the building."

"Well — I know this sounds weird — but I've never tried one before. I don't know how to do it."

"Come on — I'll teach you."

"Okay." This wasn't exactly what I'd had in mind. But at least it was better than sitting with chairs between us, not saying a word. I hoped I wouldn't make a complete fool of myself.

When we finished our drinks, we saw that Gramps and Mrs. Birdwell were taking a little breather, so we took them their drinks and told them we would be out in front. They waved to us as we got on the escalator. Brady put the skateboard on the rubber railing and made little zooming noises on the way down.

"Let's go over there, where this walk joins that one," he said, pointing to the side of the building. "You'll be able to go farther."

"Okay," I said, thinking that this whole thing was sure a lot farther from the dancing I had daydreamed about.

"Are you right-handed or left-handed?" Brady put the skateboard down and put one foot on it. Then he rode around me in a little circle waving his arms. I wasn't sure if he was showing off or just trying to give me the idea from watching.

"Right-handed," I said, looking up at him. He seemed so tall, swirling around on that skateboard.

"Me, too. So you'll put your right foot in front on the deck."

"What's the deck?"

Brady laughed. "I guess I should tell you about the board." He stopped circling me, picked it up, and held it in front of him. "The top part, the board itself, is called the deck." Then he pointed to different parts of it, giving me a little lesson. I stood close to him, and I noticed he had long eyelashes. For some reason I'd never thought about guys having long eyelashes.

He flipped it over. "This piece that holds the wheels on is called the truck. And these are guard rails to protect the underside of the deck for going up curbs."

For a minute I wasn't sure what he said because I had been noticing his freckles. "Did you say going up curbs?" I laughed some nervous laughter.

"Well, you won't do that at first, anyhow. Don't worry — I'll put my foot in front of the front wheel so you won't go anywhere while you try standing on it to get your balance."

"How should I put my feet?" I looked up at him. Brady wasn't standing on the skateboard, and he still seemed a little taller than I was. He seemed very cute, too.

"Put your right foot on first, parallel to the deck. Then, when you put your left foot up, turn so you're perpendicular to the deck. Ready?"

"I guess so." I smiled at him. He grinned, and I saw that he had a retainer. I guess I hadn't noticed it before. He must have gotten his braces off recently.

Brady planted his foot in front of the front wheel. I tried to concentrate on the skateboard as I stood up on the thing. It sure was narrow. I felt like an idiot — I wobbled getting on, and the thing wasn't even moving.

"I don't think I have very good balance," I said, teetering around on it.

"It takes practice. Just keep getting on and off while I keep my foot here. Then, when you think you're ready, I'll just take my foot away, and you'll push off with your left and ride."

"Ha!" I got on and off and wobbled some more. "It's not even moving, and I can't even stand without wobbling!"

"You're getting better. That time it wasn't so wobbly."

"I don't know about this." I tried to sound cheerful, but I was afraid he'd get sick of standing around.

"Why don't you give it a try?"

"So soon?"

"Okay, look. I'll stand right next to you, and you can put your hand on my shoulder to steady yourself when you get on."

I liked that idea a lot. "Okay."

"Ready?"

"I guess so." Brady moved to the side of the skateboard, and I stood on it. "Ooops —" It started moving along, and I grabbed for his shoulder. It was nice grabbing him. Then I wobbled too much, so I jumped off. "Well, I guess I went about two feet."

"Try it again."

"Okay." I pushed off and turned my feet sideways. "Whoooaaa!" I started to fall, so I grabbed his shoulder again. This time Brady put his arm around my waist to steady me. It was wonderful. He trotted along beside me on the lawn next to the walk, and I began rolling along. "Hey, this is fun!"

"You're doing great!"

"Yiiikes!" All of a sudden the thing bounced up in the air, and I sailed off. "OH — N-N-N-NO!" My arms and legs flew all over the place.

"Whoooops!" Brady lost his balance. I crashed against his stomach, knocking him over into the grass. The next thing I knew, we had landed in a big heap on the lawn.

"I guess that wasn't so great," I muttered as I pulled my elbow out from under his knee.

"Hey, what's this?" Brady looked around — at his hand, on his pants, and then at the grass. "What are these funny little things?"

I sat there frozen, glued to the grass, staring at my press-on nails, sticking on his pants.

"There are little red things all over the place!" He started picking them out of the grass.

I was so embarrassed, I wanted to die. "They're fingernails," I croaked.

"Fingernails?" He had collected a bunch and stared at them in the palm of his hand.

"They're fake fingernails," I blurted. "I sent in for them. They're called press-on nails." I didn't know what else to do except tell him the truth.

"Oh." Brady continued picking them off his pants and out of the grass. "I don't think they're meant for skateboarding." Then he dropped a handful of them in my hand. "Here you go," he said, handing me the last one, which was stuck on his ankle.

"Thanks," I mumbled as I stuffed the press-on nails in my jeans pocket.

"You must have hit a crack in the sidewalk."

"I guess so," I agreed quickly, relieved that Brady wasn't making a big deal about my fingernails.

"But you were getting the idea —" he said, "till we crashed!" Then he yelled, "WIPE OUT!" He waved his arms around and fell back on the grass with his legs stuck in the air.

I laughed; he seemd to enjoy reliving our crash. "Well — you're still a great teacher." I still couldn't believe he hadn't laughed about my press-on nails coming off. I took a deep breath. I liked sitting close to him on the lawn. He was nice.

We decided we'd had enough of the skateboarding lesson, and we went back inside to find Gramps and Mrs. Birdwell. They weren't at the table, so Brady and I sat down. This time there weren't any empty seats between us.

"Do you see them anywhere?" Brady looked around the dance floor.

"I think so." I pointed to the right of the band. "See, over in that corner."

"Oh, yeah." Brady watched them for a few minutes. "I think my grandmother likes your grandfather."

"I think he likes her, too."

The music ended, and Gramps and Mrs. Birdwell came over to where we were sitting.

"How was your skateboard lesson?" Gramps asked.

We looked at each other and burst out laughing. Then we told them it was fun.

"Well, now, Pearl and I were talking. She told me all about how she volunteers, teaching ceramics at the Mountain View Recreation Center."

"I'm afraid I bored the poor man to death." Mrs. Birdwell chuckled.

"Not at all. In fact, I'd love to see some of the things you make. What would you think if we left the dance a little early and stopped in there on the way home?"

"I'd like to." I looked over at Brady.

"Sure. Gran has some neat stuff there."

At eight-thirty we left the dance to go to the recreation center. On the bus, Brady and I sat next to each other behind Gramps and Mrs. Birdwell. Brady told me about his older brother, Alex, who is great at everything. He gets straight A's and is the star of his soccer team.

"I'm not that good at anything," Brady said.

"I had a friend who sounds like your brother. She moved away." I smiled at him. "I hated starting junior high without her."

"I know. It's huge compared to elementary school."

I leaned a little closer to Brady so my shoulder was touching his. I couldn't believe I was sitting there with a guy, riding the bus and actually having a conversation. When I mentioned Alicia, it dawned on me again that this was all happening without her. Unbelievable.

At the recreation center Mrs. Birdwell showed us her ceramics and all the equipment to make them. She had zillions of molds. She made bowls and ashtrays and little doodads like ceramic frogs, birds, and other little animals. There was a huge ceramic turtle with tennis shoes on that I thought was really funny. Many of the ceramic things had gold paint for trim, and she was starting now on some ceramic Santas for the holiday season. There was even a Rudolph with a nose with red glowy paint. At the end of the workroom, she had hung up a little sign. It said: USE THE TALENT YOU POSSESS — FOR THE WOODS WOULD BE SILENT IF NO BIRDS SANG EXCEPT THE BEST.

Gramps got excited about that sign, and I thought it was very nice, too. Gramps even told Mrs. Birdwell three times that it was wonderful. Sometimes Gramps repeats himself, but Mrs. Birdwell didn't seem to mind. As we left the recreation center to get the bus, Gramps said, "Well, I guess we'll see you at the next dance."

"That would be lovely." Mrs. Birdwell smiled at Gramps.

"Unless —" Gramps hesitated a minute. "Would you two like to meet us for lunch next Saturday? The Leschi Lake Café is right on the bus line, and there's a nice view of Lake Washington. I haven't eaten out much since I moved here from Minnesota. It's about time I did. Right, Janie?" He glanced at me.

"Right, Gramps." I smiled and gave him a thumbs-up.

"Would you like both of us to come?" Mrs. Birdwell asked.

"We certainly would." Gramps turned to me and winked. "Right, Janie?"

"Right, Gramps," I said eagerly. Then I worried I had sounded too excited.

"How 'bout it, Brady?" Mrs. Birdwell asked.

Brady grinned. "Sure, Gran."

We agreed on the time to meet and said good-bye. On the way home on the bus, Gramps hummed the brown jug song over and over. Then he hummed another one.

"What's that song, Gramps?"

" 'In the Mood.' "

"Oh." I leaned back against the seat. I kept thinking about how I sailed along on Brady's skateboard with his arm around my waist. I felt warm all over just thinking about it.

"Pearl Birdwell is a lovely woman," Gramps said softly. He sighed and put his head back on the seat.

"Brady's cool, too," I said, thinking again how wonderful he was not to laugh when my press-on nails fell off. I would have to wait a week to see him again. It seemed like a year.

Eleven

"Then he held me around my waist while I was on the skateboard —"

"Wow." Carly's eyes got wide as she bit into her sandwich. She had hardly swallowed when she turned to everyone and announced that Brady was a seventh-grader at Lakeview. Besides Carly, Jessica Valdez, and me, we now had two new people at our lunch table. Ilonda Williams, the thin black girl who had been one of my other first F.P.'s, and Stephanie Rutlege. She was on the plump side, like Carly, and she also had braces, like Jessica. I started saying hi to her one day because she was by herself.

"Is this Brady Birdwell guy your main squeeze?" Stephanie asked, picking potato chips out of her braces.

"Well —" I felt my face get red. "We just hang around because of our grandparents."

"That skateboarding sounds pret-ty physical —" Ilonda teased.

"You guys will never believe what happened." I

started laughing just thinking about it. "We fell on top of each other, and my press-on nails came off — He was picking them off his pants —"

"Off his pants!" Carly hooted.

"Yeah, little red fingernails stuck right on his pants, in the grass — everywhere!"

"How romantic!" Ilonda cracked up. Just then the bell rang, and we all rushed for our next class. I stopped at the trash can to dump in my lunch bag.

Jessica came up behind me. "Most people would never tell anybody what really happened," she whispered. "They'd feel like a fool." She wadded up her lunch bag and tossed it in. "No wonder you have so many friends," she called over her shoulder as she ran to P.E. "You never act stuck-up."

I couldn't believe what I had heard. Me? Janie Higgins? So many friends? Jessica was pretty mixed up, that was for sure.

On Thursday, when I got home from school, Gramps was out in the yard piling up a lot of cardboard boxes by the trash cans.

"Hi, Gramps. What's all that?"

"Boxes," Gramps mumbled. I could tell something was wrong; he always gave me a cheery hello the minute I got home.

"I can see that they're boxes —"

Gramps didn't say anything. He just turned and went in the house.

"Hey! Wait up." I ran after him. Gramps was on his way up the stairs to his room. When I got to the top of the stairs, he was already in there, and the door was closed.

I knocked on the door. "Gramps? Are you all right?" I didn't hear anything so I knocked again. "Gramps? Can I come in?"

After a few minutes Gramps opened the door. I couldn't believe it. His room looked like a department store.

"Gramps? What's all this stuff?" I walked into the room, almost tripping over a bunch of bamboo baskets. "What are you doing with all this?"

"I just kept ordering," he mumbled. "I guess I got a little carried away." Gramps shook his head and pointed to all the different things piled everywhere. "These are the miracle jars, this is the Popeil pocket fisherman — it's a fishing rod — this is the Orient Express rice steamer, here are the Ginsu knives and the steak knives, this is the bamboo steamer, this is the magic vegetable peeler and the orange juice squeezer —"

"Gramps, do you even know how to cook?"

"No."

"Then why did you —"

"I guess I've always liked gadgets." Gramps moved the Orient Express rice steamer and some of the miracle jars off his bed and sat down. "The problem is, Janie" — his voice dropped so low I could hardly hear him — "the bill comes to more money than I have in my checking account."

"Oh, dear."

Gramps took out his handkerchief and blew his nose. "Your grandmother always handled the money — no one could stretch a dollar farther than she could." He sat there, looking down at the floor. I didn't know what to say, so I just kept my mouth shut.

"And we paid cash for everything — we never bought on time. They just sent me that credit card when I opened my bank account here. You see, I'm not used to the blasted thing."

Gramps looked out the window; he seemed so embarrassed. Then he turned back to me. "Most of my social security check goes into savings bonds to help with college for you and John, and I pay your mother and father a little something for my room and board. They don't want me to, but I insist." Gramps raised his voice. "George P. Bliss was never a freeloader." Then he sighed, "I have a little left over each month, but I must not have figured the cost of these gadgets right. Everything sounded so cheap in those advertisements on television."

I moved the fishing rod out of the way and sat down on the floor.

"I just don't think I can face that young fellow at the bank to cash in a savings bond so I can pay for a magic vegetable peeler, miracle jars —" Gramps eyed all the stuff, shaking his head. "What an old fool!" Then his voice got real soft, almost a whisper. "I guess I'd better call Pearl."

"Huh?"

"To tell her that our lunch is off."

"You mean we can't meet Mrs. Birdwell and Brady at the Leschi Lake Café on Saturday?"

"I invited them — so they're our guests, but now I don't have enough money to pay the bill." Gramps stuck his jaw out. "George P. Bliss will not buy lunch on credit."

"Wait!" I jumped up and ran down the hall to my room. I grabbed my bank from my desk drawer and hurried back to Gramps.

"What's that?"

"It's my bank." I opened it, took out the money, and

began counting. "Gramps, I've got nine sixty-three."

"I'm afraid that's not enough, Janie," Gramps muttered. Thanks, anyway."

"Couldn't we just tell them to order cheap food?"

Gramps shook his head. "That's rude."

When Mom called us for dinner, Gramps and I trudged downstairs. "Could we have a picnic, Gramps?" I hoped this idea might cheer him up. "We could just tell Mrs. Birdwell and Brady that we changed our mind about the restaurant — that we thought bringing sandwiches to a park would be more wonderful. We could make peanut butter and jelly."

Gramps held the banister and shook his head.

"Maybe ham and cheese?"

"Might rain," he said sadly.

By the time we dragged ourselves to the table, everyone was there, and Mom was wolfing down an enormous salad. Her reunion was only a week away.

"I'm fanished — couldn't wait for you two," she said, chomping on a mouthful of lettuce. "This is for you." She pointed to the tuna casserole.

"My favorite," Dad said enthusiastically as he and John heaped it on their plates. Gramps and I each took a puny spoonful and just picked at the stuff. You'd think we were the dieters. Mom chatted on and on about her reunion while I kept glancing over at Gramps. He seemed so upset. I felt terrible for him. I decided right then and there to go to Mom or Dad about Gramps's financial problem. I wasn't sure, but I didn't think Gramps really understood how that credit card worked, and I knew he was too embarrassed to tell them.

After dinner Mom changed into her sweats to do her brisk walking. She did that every night after she put the food away, while we were doing the dishes. I thought she looked kind of silly, walking around the block, swinging her arms with her fanny wiggling, but I never mentioned it. Dad was reading the paper in the living room, so I went to talk to him.

"Dad?"

"Hmmmmm?" He peered over the top of the paper.

"There's this problem, and I have to talk to you."

"Okay, fire away." Dad put the newspaper down, and I began to explain the whole situation.

"I had wondered what all those boxes were by the trash cans. I asked your mother and she didn't know. Of course, she's been a little preoccupied lately getting ready to go back to Indiana."

"That's for sure. But what should Gramps and I do? We're supposed to meet them for lunch on Saturday."

"That's great — a double date! Your mother hasn't been so preoccupied that she hasn't noticed you two." Dad winked.

"I guess Mom doesn't miss much, even when she does have a lot on her mind."

"She says the symptoms of falling in love are the same whether you're twelve or eighty-two, and she said she didn't have to be a nurse to see that you and Gramps had some of the same symptoms." He grinned.

I felt my face get red. Dad wasn't helping at all. I didn't want to talk about my love life! Maybe I'd talk to Mom when she got back. She always has solutions. "I'll ask Mom —" My voice trailed off.

"Janie, look, it really is simple. Since Gramps is against making a small payment on the bill each month — buying on time he calls it, then all he has to do is send the stuff back and tell the company he doesn't want it. He should make a copy of the letter and send it to the bank that handles his credit card along with a letter telling them that he has returned the merchandise and therefore isn't going to pay the bill."

"That's all?"

"Sure. People do it all the time."

"Thanks, Dad!" I ran up to Gramps's room and told him the good news. At first he was upset that I told Dad.

"I'm just an old fool," he grumbled.

"You're not, Gramps. You just had a little trouble with the math. That happens to me all the time," I said, hoping that would cheer him up.

Gramps sighed. "Well, let's go get those boxes out of the trash."

"Good idea."

Gramps and I lugged all the cartons upstairs and boxed up all the stuff. Then he wrote a letter to the company. I looked over his shoulder while he wrote it. Even though his writing was kind of spidery and wiggly like always, I could read it. The letter said:

> *Dear Sir:*
>
> *I am returning the miracle jars, the Popeil pocket fishing rod, the Orient Express rice steamer, the magic vegetable peeler, the Ginsu knives, the steak knives, the bamboo steamer baskets, and the orange juice squeezer. I am not completely satisfied.*
>
> *Sincerely,*
> *George P. Bliss*

I put my hand on his shoulder. "I think that's a very good letter, Gramps."

"I hope they don't send for the sheriff." Gramps tried

to joke about the situation, but I could see he was still a little worried.

"Dad knows about these things. It'll be okay. On Saturday morning before we meet Brady and Mrs. Birdwell for lunch, we can have Dad drive us to the post office." I picked up one of the boxes. "We can just pile these in the corner for now."

Gramps didn't say anything. He just picked up a box and piled it in the corner on top of the one I had put there.

On Saturday morning I went to Gramps's room and grabbed one of the boxes. "I'll start carrying these downstairs and ask Dad to drive us to the post office."

"I hate to burden your father!" Gramps rapped his fist on a box. "I'm responsible for this problem. I'll drive there myself."

"But you can't see well enough anymore."

"Don't remind me," he snapped.

I hurried down to get Dad's help before Gramps got more upset. Dad was great; he went right out to the garage and opened up the trunk of the car. Gramps came out, carrying a box.

"Got any more up there, Dad?" My father asked.

"A few."

"Why don't you let me get the rest?"

"I'll get 'em, thanks," Gramps muttered and went back up the stairs for more boxes.

Dad and I waited in the garage. "What's wrong with Gramps?" I whispered.

"Shhh, Janie, his pride's hurt. I don't think we should talk about it anymore."

The three of us rode to the post office without saying a word. Gramps insisted that we stay in the car while he carried all the boxes in himself. It took forever. But Dad said we should stay in the car as he asked. While I sat there I thought about the Twenty-five Best-Loved Waltzes and the press-on nails. At least we got to keep those.

I also thought about our lunch with Brady and Mrs. Birdwell — I couldn't wait!

When we got home from the post office, Mom met us at the door. She told me Stephanie and Jessica had called, and just as I headed off to call them back, she turned to Gramps.

"And, Dad, you got a phone call, too."

I turned around in surprise. I could see he was just as surprised as I was.

"I did?"

Mom smiled at Gramps. "Yes, a Mrs. Pearl Birdwell called —"

"She did?" Gramps grinned, winking at me. "Did she want me to call her back?"

"She said she wasn't going to be available and to give you the message that she and her grandson wouldn't be able to have lunch after all. She said she was very sorry."

Gramps's face fell. I think mine must have, too.

Mom tried to cheer us up. "She didn't say anything about tonight, you know. I'm sure you'll see them there just like you did last week."

But I couldn't help worrying. Maybe Brady wanted to get out of our lunch, after I had made such a fool of myself on his skateboard. Maybe he never wanted to see me again, and Mrs. Birdwell couldn't ride the bus all the way to the Leschi Lake Café by herself. Maybe I wrecked it for Gramps. What if I had ruined everything?

Twelve

After dinner, I was all ready for the dance and waiting for Gramps. He wasn't late; it's just that I had been ready for hours. I'd been trying on outfits all afternoon and finally had picked jeans and the purple and green striped shirt that I got for my birthday last year. I had on a teeny bit of lipstick, but this time I had my own regular fingernails. I was afraid I might start biting them, so, just for something to do, I got the phone book from downstairs and sat on the edge of my bed, turning the pages of the B's. I imagined calling Brady's house to find out if everything was okay. Maybe just hear his voice and then hang up. I found a lot of people named Bird, but just four Birdwells. I couldn't remember his parents' first names, and Brady had never told me the name of his street. Gramps probably knew, but I didn't want to ask him. I had never called a boy before, and I was scared. I stared at the four Birdwells and then decided calling and hanging up was a dumb idea, anyway.

"Janie?"

I jumped and slammed the phone book shut.

"I need a little advice," Gramps said, sticking his head in my door. He held out a fistful of ties. "Which one do you like?" He held them up against his white shirt.

"Hmmmm —" I looked carefully at each candidate. "It's between the red and blue striped and the maroon one with the little navy dots, I think."

Gramps held up one and then the other.

"The red and blue striped." I smiled, giving him a thumbs-up. "It makes you look dignified."

"Dignified," he repeated. "I like that." Gramps tied it on and took the others back to his room. I went with him while he put them away. "All set?" he asked, shutting the door of his closet.

"Let's go for it." I followed him down the stairs.

Mom was reading in the living room; she put the newspaper down when she saw us. "You two look wonderful!"

Gramps straightened his tie and smiled. Mom didn't mention the lipstick, and I was glad. Probably it didn't show much. But I still felt sort of silly wearing it, and I didn't need her making a big deal about it.

"I'm sure you'll have a great time with your friends," Mom said, waving as we left.

As we waited for the bus, Wendy Freed and Margy Heldring rode by on their bikes. They were both in my P.E. class.

"Don't do anything I wouldn't do!" Margy called.

"Have fun, Janie!" Wendy yelled.

"Thanks!" I waved back. But I was so embarrassed — they seemed to know exactly where I was going. That Carly — she had probably announced to the whole seventh grade about me and Gramps and the Birdwells. On Monday I knew she'd be waiting for every detail. I hoped I'd have something to tell.

The bus pulled up, and I climbed on after Gramps. He asked me who the girls were, and I told him all about the new people I was getting to know.

"You know, Gramps, when Margy said, 'Don't do anything I wouldn't do,' that's what Alicia and I always used to say to each other. It's funny — I only got that one letter from her. I guess she's all involved in everything in San Jose."

"Well, life goes on." Gramps patted my arm.

"Right," I agreed.

Gramps asked me more about the people I was getting to know at school, and I told him about who I knew in each of my classes. When I started naming them, it really took me by surprise — I actually knew a lot of people!

As we got near downtown, Gramps started shifting around in his seat. First he turned to the aisle. Then he moved toward the window, crossed his legs, and began jiggling his foot. It made the seat bounce. Our conversation had taken my mind off how worried I really felt, but when the seat started bouncing — I got nervous again.

"They probably had something important come up," I said, trying to believe it myself.

Gramps didn't say anything. We just kept riding in silence. I bit my thumbnail a little.

"Something might have been planned that Pearl forgot about," Gramps said after a while.

We got off the bus at the Westlake Mall and took the monorail to the Center. I scoped the place out for Brady in case he was hanging around outside with his skateboard, but there was no sign of him.

The Sweetnotes were playing as we rode up on the escalator. Gramps probably knew the song; he seemed to know them all, but this time he didn't hum along. We stood by the band, looking around the dance floor and waiting.

I looked up at Gramps. The minute I saw his face, I got scared. Gramps had turned chalk white, and his eyes were frozen on the corner of the room. When my eyes followed his to the corner, I felt like I had been kicked in the stomach. A handsome silver-haired man was chatting and dancing with a lady — and the lady was Mrs. Pearl Birdwell. She seemed so happy and interested in that old man!

Then I saw Brady. He was laughing his head off with a blonde girl who was wearing a leather skirt. And Brady seemed totally excited about the girl; he was waving his arms around more than usual and not even holding his skateboard.

"Gramps," I whispered, tugging on his arm. "Let's leave."

But he had already turned around. He headed for the door, and I hurried after him. We got out of there as fast as we could. I felt sick all the way down the escalator. I knew Gramps did, too. I couldn't believe they had dumped us like this! Not only was that girl with Brady really cute, but she was totally cool-looking in that leather skirt. She was probably one of the popular girls from his class at school. What a jerk I had been to think he might like me.

It started raining while Gramps and I stood on the platform, waiting for the monorail. We huddled under the shelter together — both miserable. When the monorail came, I sat by the window and looked at the rain streaking across the glass. Gramps sat next to me with his arms folded across his chest. He had his eyes closed.

I couldn't think of a single thing to cheer him up. In fact, I couldn't think of a single thing to cheer me up.

At home we each went to our room. I don't know what Gramps did in his. But I know what I did in mine. Cried.

I finally must have fallen asleep because when I heard the knock on my door, I was all mixed up. I didn't know what time it was.

"Janie? Can I come in?" Mom sounded worried.

I went to the door and opened it. Mom closed the door behind her, and I lay back down on my bed. She sat next to me.

"Honey, what's wrong?"

"Nothing."

"Why don't you tell me about it," she said quietly. "I know something has happened."

"Oh, Mom." I started crying again. "It was so awful —"

"What was awful —" Mom rubbed my forehead. "You can tell me." She pulled a Kleenex out of her pocket and handed it to me.

I wiped my eyes and my nose. "They dumped us."

"Who dumped you?"

"Mrs. Birdwell and Brady. They were at the dance with other people. Mrs. Birdwell was dancing with this nice-looking man, and Brady was obviously having a great time with a really pretty blonde girl." I blew my nose. "Gramps and I left."

"Oh, so that's it."

"They probably just hung around us until something better came along. I was so stupid to think Brady would want to be with a nerd like me!"

"I wish I didn't have to leave you two." She sounded upset.

"Huh?"

"On Wednesday, for Indiana. My high-school reunion, remember?"

"Yeah." I started sniffing again.

"You know, Janie, going back to this reunion has made me realize how the things that seem important when you're young don't really matter later. Just because someone you like doesn't like you now doesn't mean no one ever will."

"That's easy for you to say."

"Take Orville Redenbacher. He was a nerd in high school. If he liked anyone, no one liked him back, and now look at him."

"I know, he's the popcorn king of the United States." How many times had she told me this about Orville Nerd Redenbacher? "What about Gramps, Mom? He's older now, and things are just as crummy for him as they are for me."

"Dad had a wonderful relationship with my mother, and just because Mrs. Pearl Birdwell, whom I'd personally like to strangle at this moment, doesn't know a good thing when she sees it doesn't mean that he won't meet a nice lady who will really appreciate him." Mom's voice got louder — she was getting worked up. Then she started talking in her nurse voice. "Besides, Dr. Joyce Brothers says there are over 50,000 people in the world whom each person can successfully pair with."

"Except for nerds," I mumbled.

"Janie, enough of this nerd talk. I'm going to speak with Gramps now. You'll get over this, believe me."

Ha! I thought as Mom left to go talk to Gramps. I hoped she didn't have any more bright ideas for us. Her Seattle Center plan had sure gone down the toilet.

I lay around my room, thinking about that girl and

Brady. I had never been so jealous in my life. Unbelievable . . . a leather skirt. Then I decided that jealousy was a horrible, sick feeling and I tried to think about other stuff, but I couldn't. I was trying to get Brady and that girl out of my mind when I heard another knock on my door.

"What is it?" I snapped.

"Janie?" John peeked his head in my door. "I made some pizza. Want some?"

"You what?" I had avoided my creepy brother as much as possible ever since he blasted me with those Styrofoam peanuts. This was pretty weird, I thought, as I looked at the pizza. He actually seemed to be trying to be nice.

"Mom and Dad are going out. So I made this for us." John came in with the pizza on a cookie sheet.

"Did Mom make you do this? What about some for Gramps?"

"It was her idea. But I wanted to — and Gramps is asleep." He held it out.

"You forgot napkins."

"Want to watch TV and eat it? I'll get the napkins."

"Okay, I guess." I went downstairs with him. Gramps's door was still closed.

John and I watched a bunch of dumb programs. The pizza was kind of burned; he left it in too long. This was not how I wanted to spend Saturday night, but I guess it was better than being alone in my room. Also, I suppose I have to admit that John can be okay sometimes.

Watching TV with him took things off my mind for a while, but then I started worrying about school on Monday. Carly would want to know what had happened with me and Brady. I hated the idea of having to face her. It was one thing to laugh about the skateboard lesson, but this was different.

I went up to bed after "Saturday Night Live" and saw that Gramps's light was still on. His door was open a crack, so I stuck my head in his room. He was just sitting in his chair, staring at a picture of my grandmother that he had on his dresser.

"Feeling pretty awake after your nap?" I asked.

Gramps didn't answer. I thought he hadn't heard me. So I asked him again. Finally, he looked up.

"Bruzrmphem." He mumbled.

I felt terrible. Gramps had stopped wearing his teeth.

Thirteen

"Janie!" Carly waved at me from the back of the bus. Usually I was glad to see her, but not this morning.

"Hi."

"How was the dance? Was Brady there? Was it wonderful?" Just what I had been afraid of — she couldn't wait to find out.

"He was there."

"Did you go on his skateboard again? Did he hold you around your waist?"

I didn't want to tell her, but I just blurted it out. "It was awful —"

"It was?" She seemed so surprised. "What happened?"

I could hardly talk about it. I stared out the window. I'd die if Carly blabbed about this. Could I really trust her? She's like a reporter; she loves to get the facts about people and broadcast them all over the universe. I usually didn't mind it too much when she reported fun things — but this was hideous. "Carly, please don't tell anyone, okay? I'm so embarrassed."

"I won't. Cross my heart."

I looked out the window again. Then I gulped — "He was there with another girl. I should have known he'd never like me."

"You're kidding."

"I wish I were."

"You didn't talk to him at all?"

I shook my head.

"What was the girl like?" Carly asked eagerly.

"She was cute, really cute. She had blonde hair — and she was wearing a leather skirt."

"A leather skirt! They cost an arm and a leg! I hate her."

"Huh?"

"Whoever she is, I hate her." She sounded fierce.

"Okay," I agreed immediately. "I'll hate her, too." Then I grinned at Carly, and we both burst out laughing.

The rest of the way to school, Carly gave her usual report on what everyone had done over the weekend. I felt a lot better, bouncing along on the bus listening to the news. Inside, it still hurt about Brady, but not quite as bad.

Carly was great. At lunch I could tell she hadn't reported my disaster with Brady — just like she had promised. I loved her for that. And she even helped me get off the spot when Jessica asked about it. Carly just interrupted her.

"Guess what, you guys — I nominated Janie this morning for the elections."

"Me?" I was shocked. "For what? I'm not the kind of person people nominate for anything."

"Yes, you are. I did, too." Jessica smiled. "I nominated you for treasurer."

"You're kidding!" Carly squealed. "Me, too. I figured Janie was someone you could trust with the money because she's so honest."

"I can't believe you guys are serious." I laughed. "Treasurer — that's amazing. Are you sure this isn't a joke?" Everybody kids around so much at our table that it was hard to know. Just then the bell rang. We all got up to leave.

"You'll see it's for real when they hand out the ballots." Carly grinned, stuffed the rest of her cookie in her mouth, and we left for class.

The rest of the week, I thought a lot about what Carly said. I wanted to tell Mom and Dad about it, but I didn't want to take the chance if my friends were joking. I'd feel like a jerk if I told my parents and then it turned out I hadn't really been nominated. You only needed a couple of nominations to get on the ballot, so I guessed I'd know soon enough if it was for real.

On Wednesday morning, Mom was all ready to leave for Indiana. When I came down for breakfast, she was standing in the front hall with her suitcase. She kept staring in the mirror and fiddling with her hair while she waited for Dad to come down to drive her to the airport.

"How do I look, Janie?"

"Wonderful!" She really did. She had on a pretty new dress.

"Are you sure?" Mom patted her stomach. "I just couldn't get those last three pounds off."

"You really look great. You'll be the prettiest lady there."

"Oh, Janie!" Mom threw her arms around me and gave me a big kiss.

Actually, I couldn't tell the difference between how

Mom looked now and how she looked before she went on the diet. But I did think she would be the prettiest lady there. It was weird about Mom; she always made little speeches about how women shouldn't pay so much attention to how they looked, and here she was all worried about it. I guess going back to high school made Mom forget those speeches or something. Dad came down with John and she hugged the two of us and then they were on their way. Gramps didn't come down. I guess Mom had said good-bye to him upstairs. He was sad all the time now. I was so worried about him. It was as if the good times at Seattle Center had never happened.

On Friday morning, they passed out the ballots for the seventh-grade elections. When I looked at mine, my eyes almost popped out of my head. I *was* on it! I stared for a long time at that ballot. There was "Janie Higgins," plain as day in black and white. It was the first time in my life I'd been nominated for anything, and it was one of the nicest things that ever happened to me. It didn't matter that I wouldn't win.

In my art class that afternoon, we painted with water colors. I liked art; nothing I made would win any prizes, but it was fun. I started thinking about when Gramps and Brady and I went to Mrs. Birdwell's ceramic place. She was good at art. Gramps and I had liked her sign so much, the one that said, "Use the talent you possess, for the woods would be silent if no birds sang except the best." I kept thinking about this, and it seemed to me it was a little like that with friends. If I had tried to copy those popular kids who act like they're the best — hoping I'd get to be one of them — I wouldn't have a single real friend, like I have now. That first stupid plan would have had only one result: total silence!

The picture I was painting was an underwater scene with a whole bunch of brightly colored fish. When I thought about Mrs. Birdwell, I dabbed a little white paint on the head of one of the fish. Then I put some little glasses on it. Then some earrings. It made me laugh, so I fixed up all the fish that way. Pretty soon my whole picture looked like the senior ladies at the dance; only they were fish. I leaned back and looked at it. What a goofy picture!

All of a sudden it was like a neon sign went on in my head — *There's more than one fish in the sea!* If you don't catch one, there'll be other ones to catch. That's what Mom meant about those fifty thousand people!

After school I took my picture home and marched up to Gramps's room. He was just sitting around. I knew it was worse for him; he didn't have friends to nominate him and make him feel less like a reject.

"Gramps, I made this picture for you." I handed it to him. On the top I had written the caption in big letters: "THERE'S MORE THAN ONE FISH IN THE SEA."

Gramps looked at the picture. He didn't say anything, which was just as well, because I wouldn't have been able to understand him. I saw his teeth sitting on his dresser in a glass.

"The Birdwells are for the birds if they don't want us. There are zillions of ladies at that dance, Gramps, and you can just go back and find another one to like."

"Mmfhgsgthk," he mumbled.

"I'll be right back." I went down to the kitchen and got some tape and ran back to his room. Then I taped the picture over his desk. "Just think about it, Gramps. Don't give up yet. I want to go back to the next dance Saturday night."

I thought about Brady on and off the rest of the week.

Each day it seemed to bother me a little less. School was fun — and not just lunch, art, and P.E., either. Our math class was getting to go in the computer lab — I just loved clicking away on those machines!

I have to admit that I still wasn't crazy about the idea of seeing Brady again if we did go back to the dance. But I told myself, if Gramps did decide to go it would be to dance with some new ladies, and I could just watch him and ignore Brady Birdpoo (Birdpoo's the more polite way to say what Carly and I had been calling him).

On Friday, I got the shock of my life. I was in my homeroom when my teacher told me I was supposed to report to the office. I was really scared. Mom wouldn't be back until Sunday. I didn't like it that she was gone; things just weren't the same at home. I got so worried. What if something had happened to her? What if she had fainted from all her dieting, and there was no one to help her? I got to the office and went to the desk. There were a lot of people standing around. I recognized Nalita Jones, Constance Williams, a real popular girl in my math class, Norman Schwartz, who was in my language arts class, and a guy whose name was Jeremy something.

"Are you Jane Higgins?" Mr. Nikatani, the vice principal, asked.

"Yes," I gulped.

"Congratulations."

"Huh?"

"You're the second runner-up for treasurer of the seventh grade, and we'd like you to join the other first and second runners-up in representing the seventh grade on the student council."

Me. On the student council! I almost fell over.

Fourteen

Saturday I was still in heaven about the election. I kept thinking about how it had been with my friends after school on Friday. Carly, Jessica, Ilonda, and Stephanie didn't act like I had come in last — that's what second runner-up meant, since only three people ran for each office — instead, they all crowded around me and congratulated me for being on student council! I loved it. It had been amazing just to get nominated, but the fact that I was actually one of eight student council representatives for the seventh grade was beyond belief.

I couldn't wait until Mom came back Sunday so I could tell her. When I got home from school, John was in the attic of the garage.

"Beware of the blooey grunt!" he yelled.

"Beware of the new student council representative for the seventh-grade class!" I yelled back.

In a few minutes he came charging into the house while I was eating potato chips. The only good thing about having Mom gone was that the night she left, Dad, John, and I went to Safeway and filled the basket with

Doritos, Ding-Dongs, potato chips, and other good stuff we hadn't had since Mom's diet.

"Hey, Janie? What d'ya say?"

I grinned. "I'm the second runner-up for the treasurer of the class."

"Not just your room?"

"Nope. The WHOLE seventh grade. And the first and second runners-up get to be on the student council."

"Hey, that's great, congratulations." John flew out the door. "Beware of the blooey runner-up," he called over his shoulder.

He'd never know how great it really was for me to have this happen. But Gramps would. I went right up to tell him.

"Gramps." I knocked on his door.

"Mssfmekrh."

"Please put your teeth in." I looked him right in the eye. "I have something important to tell you and after I tell you I want you to talk back to me and I want to be able to know what you say." As I heard the words come out of my mouth, I realized my voice sounded like Mom's nurse voice. It was strange, it just seemed to happen.

And it seemed to work. Gramps got out of his chair and got his teeth from the dresser. I looked out the window while he put them in.

"Gramps?"

"Yes," he said quietly.

"I'm the second runner-up for the treasurer of the seventh-grade class, and the first and second runners-up go to the student council!"

Gramps held out his arms and I ran to him and he hugged me. "Congratulations!" He said it loud and clear.

"You were right, friends don't come down the chimney. I guess I just started being friendly — and people liked me!"

"How 'bout that!" Gramps seemed so proud of me. He perked right up. He sat down at his desk and leaned back in the chair, folding his hands over his stomach. "How 'bout that," he said again, chuckling. Then he sat forward. "But you know, Janie — the real victory isn't winning a spot on the student council."

"It's not?"

"You won out over being afraid. That's what really counts. Not whether you win some election."

"I didn't win. Second runner-up means I came in third — out of three." I laughed. "I came in last, Gramps."

"The victory is in the struggle!" Gramps exclaimed.

Gramps seemed so sure. All I knew was that I couldn't wait to be on the student council.

Then he pointed at the fish picture I had taped over his desk. "Uh — Janie, I think maybe you're right about something, too." Gramps tapped the picture. "I've been looking at those fish —"

"Yes?" I said, hopefully.

"Well — now — uh — how would you like to be my date for the dance tomorrow?" Gramps asked; he seemed sort of shy about it.

But I wasn't shy. "I'd love it!" I yelled.

But as I was getting ready for the dance, I got nervous. What would I really do if Brady was there? Ignore him? Hide out in the bathroom while Gramps tried to meet some new ladies? Maybe I should act casual. Try to get an attitude like, "Eat your heart out, Birdpoo — I'm a student council rep." I had to laugh because even though a lot of times I'm not as scared as I used to be, I'm still not Miss Confidence, either. Hiding in the bathroom was more like what I'd really do.

Then, while I was fixing my hair, it suddenly hit me — *Gramps was going back to the dance because of what I'd said.* It was incredible — I was actually the person making something happen. That's what Mom always did — and Alicia, too. Following along sure was safer, I thought. If tonight was a disaster for Gramps — I'd feel horrible!

Then I remembered what he said this afternoon about how trying was what really counted. But would he really feel that way if, when he tried again tonight, the ladies were stupid and no one would dance with him? Just the thought made me more nervous than I already was.

I tried not to think about this when Gramps, Dad, John, and I went to McDonald's for dinner. Sometimes when I get nervous, I can't eat much. I guess I calmed down because besides a Big Mac, I had two orders of fries. After we were through eating, Dad dropped Gramps and me off at Seattle Center.

"Thanks for the ride, Dad." I got out and held the door open for Gramps. It takes him a few minutes to climb out, so while I waited, I quickly scanned the sidewalk and the parking lot. No sign of anyone we knew.

"You're a fine chauffeur. Thank you." Gramps shut the car door and we stood on the sidewalk for a minute and just looked at each other while Dad drove away. Then we looked at the Center House.

"Well, guess we might as well give it another try." Gramps straightened his tie.

"Right." I hoped I sounded cheerful, but all I could think of was trying to run for the ladies' room the minute we got there.

Riding up the escalator, I could tell Gramps was jittery.

First he put his hands in his pockets, then he took them out, then he put them back in.

"There's more than one fish in the sea," I whispered, praying it was true.

Gramps smiled a nervous little smile. When we got off the escalator, the Sweetnotes seemed to be taking a break. Everyone was milling around. Suddenly, we saw them. Gramps and I both stopped dead in our tracks. But before we could figure out a strategy, Brady and Mrs. Birdwell had spotted us. They waved and smiled and walked right toward us.

"George!" Mrs. Birdwell called out to Gramps. She walked right up to him. Brady stood next to her. "We missed you so much last week. Brady and I were so disappointed, weren't we, dear." She gave Brady a poke.

"Yeah." Brady grinned. Then he quickly looked away; first at the ceiling, then at the floor.

Mrs. Birdwell put her hand on Gramps's arm. "I hope you got my message about lunch. My brother came to town unexpectedly, and we had a family get-together."

"Oh?" Gramps began to perk up.

"I so hoped to see you at the dance. My brother Harry came and Brady's cousin Corinne; we had a lot of Birdwells around that night. I wanted to introduce you."

His cousin! I wouldn't have to spend the night in the bathroom after all! Just then the band started up.

"Would you care to dance, Pearl?" Gramps looked better than he had in weeks.

Brady put his hands in his jeans pockets and looked at the ceiling. Then he said casually, "Want another skateboard lesson?"

"Great." I laughed. "I was afraid, after the last time, my career as a boarder was over."

"No way." Brady stopped looking at the ceiling and smiled at me for a minute. Then we headed for the escalator.

We went right back to the same place. The sky was a dark blue and stars were out. Brady put the skateboard down near the lamppost. "Okay, just like last time, why don't you start out steadying yourself on my shoulder."

I loved that idea. I got on, held on to him, and shoved off. As we started rolling, Brady slipped his arm around my waist and trotted along beside me. I skimmed along the sidewalk while he held me. I was in heaven.

We kept practicing until it started getting cold. A few times when I started to fall off, Brady leaned close against me to keep me on. Finally, when we were really freezing, we figured we'd better go in.

Inside, we watched Gramps and Mrs. Birdwell dancing. Gramps had found a little corner where the light wasn't so bright.

"Gran wanted to call your grandfather this week to find out why he wasn't at the dance, but she didn't think it was proper for a lady to call a gentleman. Those were her exact words."

I giggled. "I almost called you. I was going to call and hang up."

"I did."

"Did what?"

"I called and hung up." Brady laughed. "Dumb, huh?"

"No — lots of people do that. Like I said, I almost did. How come your grandmother didn't tell us her brother was here when she left the message?"

"She didn't?"

"Not unless Mom forgot."

"Gran probably forgot to mention it. She was really nervous about calling in the first place."

"Brady, uh — could we go over in that corner away from the dance floor and listen to your Walkman? Then the radio wouldn't get so mixed up with their music."

"Okay."

When we got in the corner, which I had noticed was kind of dark, Brady turned on his Walkman. "I guess only one person can listen."

"Well, we could turn it upside down and sort of share it."

Brady got the idea right away. Our heads were practically touching and we each listened to an earphone. He looked out at the dance floor, then he looked at me. Then he looked at the dance floor, then he looked at the floor. "Uh — dance?" His voice caught in his throat and he kind of croaked.

"Sure." I tried to sound casual, hoping I'd remember right how Gramps showed me your arms went. I tried to seem cool as I put my left hand on his shoulder and felt him put his arm around me while we held the Walkman up, but my heart was pounding. KZOK wasn't coming in so well, so Brady tuned in Magic 108. It was playing oldies music from the seventies. At first we clowned around and pretended we were like the other dancers.

"Those Sweetnotes are awesome!" Brady let go of me, jumped back and pretended to be playing the trumpet. "I'm Jerry Sweeeeeeeney!" he said, jumping around.

"PENNSYLVANIA SIX FIVE OH OH OH!" I yelled. Then we laughed, and then we just danced, real slow. We danced and danced.

When the last song was over, we didn't let go. Then

Brady moved his head. Then he stepped on my foot. First his mouth hit my nose. But then we got it right.

Gramps and I didn't say much as we rode home on the monorail. I leaned my head back against the seat and went over every wonderful moment of the evening. I could hear Gramps humming away to himself. He looked so happy.

Before we went in the house, I whispered, "Brady kissed me."

Gramps sighed. "The first girl I ever kissed was Doreen Norville, behind her father's barn in Minnesota. I was twelve."

"Just like me."

Gramps nodded. We tiptoed into the kitchen so we wouldn't wake everybody up. I got out the bread and Gramps got out the peanut butter. "I'll never forget the first time I kissed Gramma. Not behind a barn, either. It was in a 1929 Pierce Arrow."

"What's that?" I took a bite of my sandwich.

"A car. They don't make 'em any more." Gramps looked sad for a minute. "They don't make 'em like Gramma anymore either. But you know, Janie —" he said, brightening up, "they still make pretty good ones." Then he leaned across the table. "I gave Pearl a little kiss, too," he whispered.

"I'm glad we went back there." I smiled. "I'm glad we took a chance, Gramps."

Fifteen

On Sunday, Mom got back from her reunion. While she was unpacking, I told her all the news. She was so happy about Gramps and Mrs. Birdwell she got kind of choked up. I didn't tell her all the details about me and Brady, but I did tell her everything about the election.

"And, Mom, I thought maybe it was a joke. Even though my new friends are nice, I thought I was still a nerd, but I got nominated and it wasn't a joke. And then, even though I came in last, I got to be something."

Mom had finished unpacking and she sat next to me on the bed. "That just goes to show you, you never can tell about people. Sometimes when you don't think you're much of anything, you can end up being very successful."

"Yeah, I know, 'take Orville Redenbacher for instance' — how was it to have the popcorn king of the United States at the reunion?"

Mom got a strange look on her face. Then she turned bright red. She cleared her throat and in a funny little voice said, "He was the wrong Orville Redenbacher."

"Huh?"

"The Orville Redenbacher in my class —" she blurted, "isn't the popcorn king —" Then she began giggling. "There must just be more than one Orville Redenbacher in the state of Indiana."

"Not the popcorn king?" I couldn't believe it. I started laughing my head off. "He's NOT the popcorn king!"

Mom cracked up. Then after a while she caught her breath and just kept shaking her head. "To think all this time it was the wrong Orville Redenbacher —"

I stared at Mom. Mom stared at me. Then we both burst out laughing.

That afternoon John announced that Gramps had helped him with a new stupid pet trick that was sure to get Juliet on the David Letterman show. He insisted that the whole family watch, so after lunch we all trooped out to the front yard. Mom, Dad, and I stood in a row by the steps. There was no sign of John.

"Here we go again," I said disgustedly.

Just then we heard John. *"Da-da-da-da-da-da-da-da — Da-da-da-da-da-da —"* He was singing — if you could call it that. But we still couldn't see him. I looked at Mom and rolled my eyes.

Then John and Gramps came around the corner, pushing Juliet sitting in John's old wagon. I couldn't believe it. She was dressed up like Batman, with a little black mask with ears, and she was wearing a long blue cape. The wagon was painted black. I guess it was supposed to be the Batmobile. They had some kind of gadget with wires next to her in the front of the wagon.

"Batman! That's great!" Dad cracked up.

"Da-da-da-da-da-da-da-da —" John sang again.

Juliet's paw hit the gadget, which started a tape. "BATMAN!" it sang out.

Mom and Dad clapped all over the place, yelling "Hooray!"

I clapped several polite claps. Gramps must have helped John rig up the tape recorder that went "BAT-MAN" when Juliet's paw pushed it. That actually was pretty neat.

"More! More!" Mom and Dad cheered and clapped.

"Want us to do it again?" John beamed.

Then while Gramps was rewinding the tape recorder, Juliet suddenly leaped out of the wagon.

"Oh, no!" I screamed. It was the mailman! Juliet charged toward the gate, her cape flying. She lunged her head through the fence, barking and growling like mad.

The mailman stopped, frozen in his tracks. He stared in disbelief at Juliet, baring her teeth and jumping around in her cape wearing that black mask with its bat ears. Then he started turning red, yelling, and shaking his fist. "YOU PEOPLE ARE CRAZY!"

We stared at him, speechless, from behind the fence.

"YOU'RE ALL LUNATICS — THE WHOLE FAMILY!" Then he spun around and tore down the street.

"He'll never deliver here again," I said.

We just looked at each other. I don't know who started laughing first — maybe Gramps. But we all started to crack up, so we ran into the house, where the mailman wouldn't hear us. John dragged Juliet, but it took him forever to get inside; he kept tripping over her cape.

Before she shut the back door, Mom watched the mailman disappear down the block. "I'll talk to him when things calm down," she said in her nurse voice. Knowing Mom, she probably would fix it up.

The whole thing about the mail made me think about Alicia. I hadn't heard from her for ages — but I hadn't written, either, I realized. So I decided to go up to my room and write her.

Dear Alicia,
How is California? I bet you're having a great time. I sure am! The seventh grade is really wonderful now. I didn't mention it before because I wanted to write happy letters, but I was miserable at first. Now I have some new friends, Carly Reese, Ilonda Williams, Jessica Valdez, and Stephanie Rutlege. They're the crowd I hang around with, but I know a lot of other people, too, some not as well — just to say hi to. I can't wait for you to meet them when you come for a visit at Christmas. And guess what? I was nominated for treasurer of the seventh-grade class. I didn't win, but I was second runner-up, and the runners-up get to represent the whole seventh grade on the student council. I know it's not as big a deal as winning something and being a class officer, but it sure makes me happy. The most exciting news is that Brady Birdwell, the guy I told you about who goes to Lakeview Junior High, well, I was at the senior citizens dance Saturday night with Gramps again and Brady kissed me! Well, don't do anything I wouldn't do! Ha! Ha! CAN'T WAIT TO SEE YOU AT CHRISTMAS!!!!

Love,
Janie

Then I thought for a moment and decided to add a little more.

P.S. Not everything in the letters I wrote before was exactly true, I exaggerated. But everything in this letter is absolutely true!

P.P.S. I think I love Brady Birdwell.